BRIAN BELTON

ALBION'S
ROCK

First published 2014 by DB Publishing, an imprint of JMD Media Ltd, Nottingham, United Kingdom.

ISBN 9781780914299

Brian Belton
ALBION'S ROCK

Land of Hope & Glory

Victory

Sheagle Wright looked out onto the world through a window of power. The crowd at the top of Downing Street were still cheering and calling for another appearance. All past coalitions, deals and mergers aside, she was the first Liberal Prime Minister in modern history. What risk she had taken weaning her party away from the old 'Democratic' adjunct had been vindicated; that meaningless appendage had weighed the Party down since the last quarter of the twentieth century. 'People don't want democracy, they want leadership!' That had been the war-cry that had taken her a long way from her days as a rebellious, but intellectually precocious East London school kid, who, because she had no dad, because she was female and 'mixed heritage', was given no chance, right from the start. But 'Little Shelly', as her mum had always called her, had proved them all wrong and now she was the most powerful person in England, still the most sovereign of all the States of the CEE (Confédération des États d'Europe).

As she gave her shining, almost silver smile to those who celebrated her accession, she had every intention to use her authority and influence without seeking anyone's permission or forgiveness. She had analysed her own ambition and knew her motivation as she might a child within her.

It wasn't, like so many before her, a lust or a hunger almost for its own sake. For Sheagle it was a want to be in a place or position where she could best express herself. Power was just the raw material, the granite, out of which she could sculpt her own creations. That was her desire, to be able to stand back and look at what she had done. But she understood that at that point she would reshape it again. Perfection for Wright was to be found in constant movement and change; it was the firework show of human adaptation that elated her and she wanted to be at the centre of the fountain of flame, to feel she was the spark that ignited the whole performance. If she had a faith, it was in humanity's innate propensity to create as demanded. That was the fulcrum of her art and the point of her focus and effort, the work that made her feel alive; her joy.

This is why, and the sharp point of how, the Prime Minister had dragged her formally beleaguered party into the ground lost by the painfully flaccid Tories over the years. At the politically tender age of 23, in her first speech to the Party Conference, she had attacked the Democratic 'tag-on' (as she called it). It was this critique that had been instrumental in seeding her infamy:

England has never been a democracy and it is unlikely it will ever be a democracy. That would mean that the State would be run for the people, by the people... all the people. But I, you, we are all subjects of His Britannic Majesty. He is the embodiment of the State, not some vague and amorphous mass which no one can clearly identify; a foolish notion that we are all somehow, or that we even want to be, the same thing, or indistinguishable as one ant might be from another.

The massive Olympic Stadium erupted in a great approving roar. She yelled through the mist of the noise;

Here, in 'our' England, the vote is not a 'right'; it is a privilege, given by His Majesty's Government. It is a gift of the State which allows subjects, once every six years to make a mark on a piece of paper, indicating who they would like, from a limited set of alternatives, to be the voice and the muscle of the monarchy – that is what we are part of, a monarchical state. There are no citizens in this 'our' England! We are something more, an entity writ in history and destiny. This realm, 'our' island fortress, is no commonplace republic.

She spat the last word out like a poison as another huge wave of sound tore into the dusky, darkening summer sky and the chant that she had given to the party exploded from the din; *'Our* England! *Our* England!' Again her voice sliced through the clamour;

*So the lessons in 'citizenship' that creep through our schools are exercises in deception. The only lesson about citizenship that is needed is that there are no citizens within the bounds of **our** shores and as such we have no inalienable rights. So, demanding rights is a waste of time. It is the King who by his grace bestows and withdraws so called rights. It is He who has a responsibility for His realm and we have duties to him. But we rarely hear about people 'demanding their duties'!*

The hollering collapsed into tumultuous laughter.

*The first lesson in being a subject of **our** England is that the Prime Minister of this country is the governing mouthpiece of the King. That's why we don't need a vote to go to war or anything else for that matter. The Prime Minister acts on behalf of the King, who the government advises. It is very simple. He is us and we are Him. He is England, WE ARE ENGLAND!*

The 250,000 people in the Stadium were on their feet, but the close to a million people watching her on the great electronic monitors that surrounded the colossal edifice, vastly extended since it hosted its second Zargon Enterprises Olympiad ten years earlier, caused the very ground to vibrate with stamping and cheering.

Hence to 'be' a democrat (she sneered as she screwed that word out of herself) would be the same as being a traitor, someone who commits treason! We don't want 'good citizens' we want 'loyal subjects' because a loyal subject is a good subject. A disloyal subject is a traitor. A loyal subject does their duty to the King and in doing that undertakes their duty to their country, and so to themselves and those they love. That is what this country needs to become, a better place for everyone to live in. We need to do more to reward those who do their duty by giving them privileges and spend less time talking to people about imaginary rights they think they should just 'have' on demand whilst doing nothing in return...'ENGLAND EXPECTS EVERY MAN TO DO HIS DUTY!!'

The cheers thundered reply.

I am a loyal subject. I WILL do MY duty. Will you?

The 'YES!' seemed to shake reality.

I am not a traitor! ARE YOU?

The 'NO!' turned the stadium into an eruption of volcanic sound.

Over the cityscape, from the river to beyond the marshes, the atmosphere was filled first with the resounding affirmation, followed to the final question a thunderous negation.

This clear, aggressively passionate and forthright style grabbed headlines and the attention of the media. There was of course a shrill outcry from the collective left and shivers of fear ran through the echelons of the old guard of the Party, disassociations were swift in coming. But the honesty and courage of the *New Guinevere* as *The Solar* proclaimed her, together with her intelligence, strength and beauty, appealed to the public. The entire package pushed Sheagle to the fore amongst the shabby, directionless political hippies that had been the Liberal Democrat Party. It seemed that she had given 'being English' a meaning and a distinctiveness; she had resurrected, or more realistically invented a form of redoubtable and defiant identity that reverberated deeply in the popular psyche.

A follow up interview in *The Solar* resulted in her suspension from the Party;

The world has never seen a democratic empire. Democracies are always weak, short lived affairs, directed by the lowest common denominator, and don't point me towards the United States where 'all the people' actually do not take part in a democratic process. America is an oligarchy headed up by people who are the most able to pay to be elected. A mishmash of cronyism founded on 'old money' and dividends from financing foreign conflicts from the First World War on. It was American industry that underwrote the rise of Hitler with the long-term aim of undermining the British grip on the oilfields of the Middle East. When did the American people vote for that?

In England our head of state is born and reared to rule from a tradition and bloodline going back over millennia! We need to celebrate that purity and stop apologising for it!

Lazavision and net-sonic interviews followed in an avalanche of media excitement. Her flashing white teeth and long shapely legs graced every chat show and lowbrow current affairs slot for weeks. Viewers loved her brash, clever and often hilarious candidness. As such it was not long before Wright was not only returned to the political fold, but became the star and saviour of her Party.

At the same time Sheagle attracted a new breed of people from within and outside the Liberal pond. People like Gwendolyn Jebb and Malcolm Craven rallied to her cause and summarily transformed an impotent group of whining do-gooders and bleeding hearts into a force that would not be pushed around by the antiquated regulations of Parliament.

Sheagle was the first queen of right-wing politics since Margaret

Thatcher, but Ms' Wright was a very different prospect to the Iron Lady who had led her country into what had become a forgotten South Atlantic scuffle with a then partially industrialised, financially and spiritually bankrupt, socially amoral South American State. At just 33 Sheagle was of the people, the East End girl made good. She still spoke in a cockney accent, albeit in the more genteel tones of her West Essex borderland roots. The *Plaistow Princess* (as some of those who rose with her occasionally referred to her, behind her back) preached a kind of working class pragmatism that appealed across England's ossifying class landscape. This, together with her Marilyn Monroe figure, jet black hair that fell down to the middle of her back, icy blue eyes and the lightly bronzed complexion of her Gypsy father, were perhaps the most potent weapons in her Party's landslide election victory. This triumph that had made the Labour/ Conservative alliance that had been ranged against her look like a moribund and toothless opposition that they in fact were.

She returned to her desk. Sheagle was going to name her cabinet the next day; as usual her judgments would be made without consultation or hesitation. She followed the dictum of the Samurai, making her decisions in the space of seven breaths. Shelly grabbed the congratulatory message from her predecessor as Leader of the Party, the satin skinned public school boy whom she had pilloried as 'might-be mouse' during her campaign to seize control of the Party. She turned the frosty "well-done" over and began to scribe the names of, what she was to call, her 'Board of Management' on the blank side. She froze for something less than a second before writing the first name in her fine hand. 'Malcolm Craven'; the new Member of Parliament for Preston North and former Special Air Service captain. For Wright the rest of her cabinet grew out of this decision. Within minutes she was ready for the next morning's press conference, where she would make public the names of the small group of men and women who she would use to take England into what she foresaw to be a new era.

At the time of Wright's announcement about the make-up of her cabinet and her intentions regarding Gibraltar, Severiano Casillas was laying naked on the soft white bed in his lover's apartment. He was smoking his second cigarette after a particularly protracted and passionate interlude. A slight, cool breeze wafted through the three-quarter drawn curtains, its vague sweet spiciness reminding him of the Madrid streets that surrounded the apartment block. For a moment his mind pondered on how the incoming air merged with the smoke he exhaled. He listened, seemingly half interested, to the English Prime Minister. He watched her, a ghostly figure as the sunlight penetrated the three dimensional figure painted into the room via the old lazavision monitor. Her slight movements stirred him, the way she half smiled at the response of her audience. Her audaciousness appealed to him; he could understand the kick she was getting. He let a hint of a smile onto his face, apparently returning Wright's gesture.

A motion of the curtains caught his attention and he watched them for some minutes as they fluttered slightly and then stilled. He stubbed out his not yet half finished cigarette and turned his gaze towards the figure sleeping next to him. He pondered at the dune like curves of the pale body that lay almost lifeless on the sheets that smelt of their sex. He would make love just once more and then he would have to contact his Prime Minister – who he knew would be in a roaring rage at that woman's words, but they were just words after all.

A new dawn

Wright marched along the corridors of St James's Palace. Her slim but powerful legs glided her 5 feet 10 inch frame on with extensive, forceful but elegant strides. At exactly 9am, she made her entrance into the press-room with all the arrogance of a diva, to meet the collective ranks of the international news media head on. There were not too many surprises as she attached names to the various responsibilities most central to her team. There were two posts left to fill before Sheagle drew breath to announce, "Ladies and Gentlemen, one person will take the role of Deputy Prime Minister and Minister of Defence, as I believe, over the next few years, the responsibilities of these posts will be intimately related." There was a mumble in the room before Wright attached Craven's name to the titles. This was followed by perhaps half a second of silent incredulity, succeeded by an audible collective intake of breath. Sheagle smiled at the response.

Craven was still, in his fifty-fifth year, a striking man. Although his blonde hair had hints of grey, his six-foot, trim and fit body looked good in the T-shirts and jeans he chose to wear most of the time. He had been a lazavision presenter before being selected to represent the Party.

Over a number of years Craven had fronted a day-time programme that took groups of viewers – shop assistants, telephone sales people and so on – to remote islands or mountain tops and turned their struggles not to die into entertainment for bored pensioners, indolent students, truants and the jobless. However, he was a surprise choice for the popular political monitor programme *'Time for Answers'* when the European Broadcasting Company sacked its long time host, Finlay Black. It was in the throes of hot-debate during *'T4A'* that Craven had confronted the Labour Deputy Prime Minister, Paul Prosket, about the then government's intended handover of the 'administration' of Gibraltar to the Spanish, disregarding a referendum of the Rock's population that had overwhelmingly voted not to accept rule from Madrid. Craven had effectively accused the DPM and the Labour government of treason and of being openly acting against the 'King's subjects in the Mediterranean'. The tabloids fell on this encounter in particular and the issue in general like carrion; it became the start of the campaign to force the government into an early election and its panicky coalition, cobbled together with the hapless Tories to face the force of nature that was Wright.

Sheagle counted her breaths as the consternation gathered momentum. One, two, three, "It will be Mr Craven's first duty to revisit recent decisions regarding the sovereignty of Gibraltar, which whilst my government has any say in matters whatsoever, will remain under the rule of His Majesty".

The previous hubbub was gone. Its place was filled by a tirade of shouted questions and the flashing of dozens of attempts to catch the moment. Prime Minister Wright raised her voice, her deep East End tones rang out in warning and with authority: "Let me say here and now. Gibraltar is English territory! It is '**Albion's Rock**' and as such, as much as any part of this realm, is under the protection of His Majesty. Any incursion of its borders will be met with all the force that this country can muster. The flag of England flies over **our** Rock and that standard will be defended to the hilt. Let it be known the red and white stands as a fair warning against any foreign incursions." The questions, although they kept coming were diluted with "Oh my God's", some incredulous laughter, several "No's" and one very obvious "Fucking Hell!"

Gib

The majority of people in the British Crown Colony of Gibraltar were not taking in Sheagle's historic performance. As Wright's words went rippling out across the globe, there were people on the Rock who by accident or design were watching the right lazavision station or listening to the net-sonic who would quickly spread the word before the collective official media would bring something like the full impact of the new British Government's declared policy with regard the Rock to the attention of the most Gibraltarians. With the portrait of His Britannic Majesty, Gibraltar's monarch looking on, his local representative, Governor, Conception Etxberria was one of a minority transfixed and hanging on every word the West Ham woman uttered, as the press core went ballistic. Daniel Jimenez, the Chief Minister of the Council of Ministers, was staring at Sheagle from an identical black leather easy chair to the one Etxberria sat on the very edge of, next to him. Jimeneze swallowed what was left of his glass of fine malt. After a second he muttered, "We need to talk to the Assembly". There were 17 members of the House of Assembly, representing the population's local interests. Of that number 15 were elected. The ex-officio members were the Attorney General and the Financial and Development Secretary. England was responsible for defence and foreign affairs. Conception looked hard at Jimenez for a few expressionless seconds. "What will we say?" she asked in the soft accent cultivated within her aristocratic Anglo-Spanish background. "I don't know." Confessed Jimenez, "But we need to talk, or get people together soon… now in fact."

Almost from the moment Sheagle mentioned Gibraltar the Euro, that had been overwhelming the Dollar on the money markets for almost a year, fell dramatically against the American currency. The price of oil, that had been stable for months, rose immediately by $375 a barrel. This was no bad news for England. The country had been a net exporter of oil for decades, while shale had made the nation autonomous in terms of gas, now used to fuel more than 50 percent of motor vehicles. But recent exploitation of the huge gas and oil fields surrounding the Falkland Islands, together with the extensive black subterranean sea about to be tapped around Isle of Man and in the Wash, would push 'Wright's Realm' (as 'The Solar' was now calling the nation) into the top five oil producers on the planet.

Arimatheans

Wright's referral to 'Albion' caused more than a few ears to be pricked for a range of reasons. What some called the 'Cult of Albion' the 'Arimatheans' had its organised origins in the mid-Twenty-First century, but its roots went back to the earliest social foundations of England. The sect had gained something akin to a Masonic identity over the previous twenty years. While the numbers involved were unknown, it was thought this faction of Anglicanism, which centred on an idea of the spiritual essence of England represented in the figure of the Arch Angel Albion, could be numbered at between several hundred thousand and a couple of million members or adherents. However, there was a general feeling that the movement had been growing since the start of the most recent political tension between England and Spain, or at least its profile was more obvious as a fundamentalist response to the evermore lax interpretation of mainstream Christianity.

What more than a few commentators had taken to be quite a dangerous cult was thought to include many from the influential elite within the media, academia, politics and the military, some as faithful adherents others as pragmatic affiliates. There was also perhaps a sizable group just looking for an alternative to religopolitical stance of 'The Festival', which although a potent force as the voice of the See of Canterbury, refused to become openly involved in seeking political power.

The Arimatheans described themselves as being privy to a primal spiritual energy found in the merging of Christian mysticism and mythical representations of Englishness. This was personified in female archetypes that embodied the qualities of the Arch Angel Albion (AAA for some of the devotees). These exemplary characters were at least promoted as spiritual role models, but at extreme wings of the cult they were sanctified as Saints might be in Catholicism and made the focus of adoration. This extreme faction was associated with idioms championing the English as a 'chosen people' and 'inheritors of the earth' via a 'sacred crusade'.

The Arimatheans believed that the Angelic figure of Albion was a heavenly feminised incarnation of Joseph of Arimathea, a wealthy disciple of Christ, who, according to the book of Matthew 27:57-60, asked Pontius Pilate for permission to take Jesus' dead body in order to prepare it for burial. He also provided the tomb where the crucified insurrectionist (as Jesus was understood to be by the Cult) was laid until his Resurrection. Joseph is mentioned a few times in parallel passages in Mark, Luke and John, but nothing further is heard about his later activities. However, apocryphal legend has it that he accompanied the Apostle Philip, Lazarus, Mary Magdalene and others on a preaching mission to Gaul (an area encompassing contemporary France, Luxembourg and Belgium, most of Switzerland, the western part of Northern Italy, as well as the parts of the Netherlands and Germany on the west bank of the Rhine). Lazarus and Mary stayed in Marseilles, while the others travelled north. At the English Channel, St Philip sent Joseph, with twelve disciples, to establish Christianity in the most far-flung corner of the Roman Empire: Albion (the most ancient name by which England has been known). The year AD 63 is commonly given for this 'event', hence the numerological alternative to the letter 'A' as symbol for the Arimatheans (being the first letter of 'Albion' and 'Arimathea') was the number '9' (6 + 3).

According to legend Joseph achieved his wealth in the metals trade, and in the course of conducting his business, he probably became acquainted with England, at least the south-western parts of it. Cornwall was a busy tin mining district and well-known in the Roman Empire for this metal that was essential to their military machine, while Somerset was renowned for its high quality lead. The Arimatheans believed that Joseph was the uncle of the Virgin Mary and therefore a great uncle of Jesus, and that he brought the Christ boy along on his business trips to Albion. Hence the words of Blake's famous hymn, Jerusalem:

And did those feet, in ancient time,
walk upon England's mountains green?

This was said to be the reasoning behind sending Joseph on the first mission to England, and why it was seen as appropriate that he should come initially to Glastonbury, that gravitational centre of legendary spiritual activity in the West Country. The Arimatheans gave credence to the legend that Joseph sailed around Land's End and headed for his old lead mining haunts. Here his boat ran ashore in the Glastonbury Marshes and, together with his followers, he climbed a nearby hill to survey the surrounding land. Having brought with him a staff grown from Christ's Holy Crown of Thorns, he thrust it into the ground and announced that he and his twelve companions were "Weary All". The thorn staff immediately took miraculous root, and it is alleged that the tree that grew from it can be seen there still on Wearyall Hill.

Joseph met with the local ruler, Arviragus (another 'A', or 'alpha') and soon secured himself twelve hides of land at Glastonbury on which to build the first monastery in Britain. From here he became the country's evangelist.

Much more was added to Joseph's legend during the middle ages. He was gradually inflated into a major saint and cult hero, as well as the supposed ancestor of many English monarchs. He was said to have also brought with him to England a cup used at the Last Supper, which was deployed to catch the blood dripping from Christ as he hung on the Cross. A variation of this story is that Joseph brought with him two cruets, one containing the blood and the other the sweat of Christ. Either of these items is known as 'The Holy Grail', the object(s) of the quests of the Knights of King Arthur's ('A' again) Round Table. One legend goes on to suggest that Joseph hid the Grail in Chalice Well at Glastonbury for safekeeping.

According to the Arimatheans, Albion arose in mortal form in eras wherein England was threatened or in need of regeneration. According to Arimathean theology Joseph of Arimathea had in fact been a woman and mother of Baer (also the name of the daughter of Boudica, the warrior Queen of the Iceni) the female forebear Ygerna, who three centuries later would give birth to the boy who would be King Arthur.

The Arimatheans maintained the male persona of Joseph came from her having been brought up as a boy, her father wanting to pass his wealth on to his only child, but knowing that she would have been disallowed from trading in those ancient times because she was not male. As such, the Arch Angel Albion was a female figure and all her mortal incarnations were women; these included mythological characters like Guinevere, Maid Marion and Britannia alongside historical figures such as Boudica, Baroness Thatcher, Eleanor of Aquitaine, Julian of Norwich, Elizabeth I and Queen Victoria.

However the Arimatheans had it that the first spiritual manifestation of the 'English soul' was Britannia, who inspired the constant guerrilla warfare against Roman occupation of England and was eventually to become a goddess in Roman Britain. It was believed Britannia was embodied in Boudica, who led a rebellion against Rome around the time that Joseph of Arimathea was bringing Jesus to England. As such the Arimatheans believed that Britannia was the precursor of Albion, a sort of John the Baptist equivalent, whose role it was to 'prepare the way'. Other historical figures were implicated by the Arimathean credo, such as Henry VIII, Robin Hood, St George, Winston Churchill, Oliver Cromwell, Montgomery of Alamein and Alfred the Great. These individuals were understood as manifestations of Arthur and as such agents (or 'sons') of Albion. Sheagle's 'call to Albion' immediately provoked speculation about her involvement with the Arimatheans, and led not a few adherents to begin to see her as a possible embodiment of the Arch Angel and sacred mortal incarnation of England.

Green & Pleasant Land

Parliament

The Liberal majority in Parliament, over all other parties, amounted to twenty-two seats. However, just as the majority of 'Lions' (as they had called themselves after adopting an image of a lioness pouncing into action at Sheagle's first conference as leader, nearly three years prior to the Party's rise to power) had usurped the traditional political territory of the Tories, a sizeable minority had adopted the ground left vacant by the demise of socialism. As such, about forty Liberal MPs could not be relied upon to follow Sheagle and Craven along the more radical paths they fully intended to tread.

The implementation of proportional representation had allowed the Liberals to gain a solid foothold and then dominate Parliament in the space of two elections, but it had also brought a whole gaggle of other interests into active political contention and reinforced other groups. The Scottish Democrats, Welsh Nationalists, the various Irish factions, the English National Party and the Ecology Coalition had a collective representation of over sixty seats. Although a diverse group, the nature of the new Parliament and the Government's ambitions together necessitated a level of consultation with what the popular media had dubbed 'The Militia'.

It was Gwendolyn Jebb's first job as Home Secretary to start a 'dialogue' with these political forces. No one envied her the task, but Gwendolyn was certainly the person for the task. A gold medal from the Cape Town Olympics, where she had captained the English Speedway team from no-hope outsiders to an epic victory over the allconquering Japanese, was testament to her ability to pull people together and motivate them. She had tremendous intelligence sharpened with reptilian guile. At the same time, whilst holding with the buccaneering spirit of her leader, Gwendolyn was the Party's supreme tactician, having marshalled it to first a landmark election, followed three years later by complete victory at the polls. Gwendolyn was the dynamo of the Party machine and it was no secret that she relished the challenge. As such she had started about her current labours long before the first ballot had been cast.

Freddie Williams was the least complicated of Jebb's opponents. He had been well satisfied by the promise of a fully independent Wales in the Liberal election manifesto. Davie Howard needed something more. Scotland, already a semi-independent state, entered into the bargaining demanding its own place within the economic decision making struc-tures of Europe and control of Scottish regiments in the European Armed Forces. However, Jebb's tour-de-force was bringing Hugh Connell and Dermot Hart together long enough to establish grounds for a new polit-ical structure in Ireland. After all sorts of overt and covert bargaining, Ulster would become a semi-autonomous, demilitarised region, having federal status within a united Ireland, but at the same time, remaining an English province.

These 'arrangements', taken together, went a long way to meeting the English Nationalist's desire for an independent English state. Roland

Edu, the leader of the ENP, was close enough to the right of the Liberal Parliamentary Party to be satisfied with the situation. He was a career politician, born into the English upper class. His family connections had boosted his profile and electoral credibility. Being the brother of the King's consort might have had negative and positive effects, but Roland had experienced only the latter. His rise correlated precisely with the monarch's courtship of and marriage to Paramicha, who herself was an extremely popular figure in the country and abroad. Edu was an intelligent but mostly inscrutable power broker. The ENP posters in the election had featured his likeness looking out over an English country landscape; his flawless ebony skin and dark, sincere eyes, set within an expression designed to show determination together with the love and pride he had for his nation, which was not Britain, but as the words under the image told:

England for the English!

Jebb would broker what in effect would be a new federated United Kingdom ('New Britain') made up of four elements. Constitutionally this was a revolutionary plan that was put through the system at a lightening rate. Within the first three months of the new Parliament, the Welsh assembly became a Parliament in its own right, whilst the Scottish Parliament adopted full federal powers. Ulster MPs took places in the Republican system. All this effectively removed the 'Militia' from Westminster. Alongside Scottish and Welsh MPs elected to what was to be the last 'British' Parliament, a representative group of English MPs were assigned to a new democratic body, the Council of the Isles, that also included representatives from the

Channel Isles, the Isle of Man, the Shetland, Orkney and the Scilly Isles, all of which had major stakes in new energy sources either in term of geography or financial involvement.

This process was speeded up by dissolution of the Upper House of Parliament and its replacement by the 'Kings Council'. The members of this body were appointed by the King, but every one of the one hundred strong Council had to be nominated by Sheagle.

All this activity obliged the Tory and Labour parties to maintain their failed electoral coalition to oppose the Liberals in Parliament, who now had a much stronger, if somewhat turbulent, majority. The opposition coalition had hoped to draw in the E-Co and the English Nationalists, but both those groupings found themselves to have too little in common to join forces.

In the space of ten months Gwendolyn Jebb had become the architect of 'New Britain'; a federated monarchy wherein the political ambitions of the 'Militia' had been satisfied at the expense of being disarmed, so making England the strongest political presence within a federation of interdependent states. However, it was dominated by a representative dictatorship, maintaining control over the vast proportion of the formerly British economic and military power.

Jebb's preparations had been thorough and what the public saw as a whirlwind transformation of the British State was in reality the culmination of nearly fifteen years of planning, negotiation, wheeling, dealing and manipulation, together some thinly disguised bribery and a little blackmail. In exchange for independence the Militia had bartered most of its muscle beyond particular borders of interest, be they Scottish, Irish, Welsh or English. For example, the resultant autonomy of England had seemingly made the ENP redundant as a political force, becoming little more than a right-wing faction of the Liberal government in the resulting English Parliament.

United States of Europe

The vast constitutional changes meant that in effect Britain was subject to cabinet rule during the months it took to make the transition. This meant that the creation of the United States of Europe (USE) went on with limited British involvement. As such, when the reformed New Britain emerged from the conversion process it looked across the North Sea at a vast infant state, still finding its feet and breaking-in its institutions. However, whilst Wales and Scotland rushed to the arms of the 'great foreign monolith' as Roland Edu had christened the USE on *T4A*, Gwendolyn Jebb told the Council of the Isles:

> *English interests lie in England and our strongest affinities are with the English speaking nations of this earth, our traditional allies with whom we have stood shoulder to shoulder throughout our history. We will look to this enduring relationship and seek to extend this family. This is why we will propose the introduction to this Council of representation from the Falkland Islands and Gibraltar.*

The gasps that resounded around the great Council chamber in Douglas amused Jebb. For her such consternation was the predictable voice of indignation that throughout her life she had ridden always to her advantage. For Gwendolyn it was a sign that she had won.

The Gibraltar Question

What had become known as 'The Gibraltar Question' had deteriorated very slowly. For several years there had been a gradual, not much more than tokenistic build up of Spanish forces around the general area of the Gibraltar frontier with Spain. The border had been more or less closed in terms of non-essential activity; this had been something of a lever that took Wright's prime ministerial predecessor to a point beyond compromise; compliance to Spanish wishes. At the same time, the Parlamento de Andalucia (the Parliament of Andalusia in Seville) had been in a state of constant uproar. The strange alliance of the strong Espano-British representation aligning with the increasing and vociferous Andalusia separatist party had continued to make loud demands for the demilitarisation of the region. The apparent growing 'active apathy' towards Andalusia (both Britain and Spain were depicted as calculable in this respect) together with the new regional autonomy that seemed to have transformed Britain, fired old antagonisms and gave rise to feelings like those expressed by the charismatic Iker Ballesteros, chair of Nacion Andaluza. In a speech to the European Parliament. He claimed also to speak for many other 'engulfed regions':

Andalusian nationalism is in solidarity against the neoliberalism that marginalises and imposes uniformity. This is nothing new, but every day it is more insistent. Cultural uniformity is trying to impose itself on the vitality of different peoples. They are trying to make us forget even who we once were.

The Andalusian people is suffering a constant assault on its identity,
and European and Spanish ways are forced upon us, which are not
our own. Some of us think that the USE doesn't care about us. As left-
wing Andalusian nationalists we believe that the best way to struggle
for human freedom in this land is to join up with others, yes including
the Espano-British, in the fight to recover our identity as a nation and
to take our place among the community of peoples and thus be able
to act in solidarity.

This sentiment seemed to be stoked up by the sudden attention being
lavished on Gibraltar by the English Government, which was a huge and
growing surprise in Britain, Spain and Europe. There was a level of jeal-
ousy and resentment amongst Andalusians at the relative negligence, in
terms of their position, by Spain and Europe relative to the consideration
the Rock was getting.

Extending

The process of bringing Gibraltar into the Council of the Isles started
with the Falklands being elected to the Council. This occurred without
much opposition, the Irish protest vote was the only movement against
the South Atlantic representation. The proposal for Gibraltar's entry was
postponed until the Council's next meeting at which the Falkland Islands
would be a voting member. The subsequent debate was made a battle by
the joint forces of the Irish and the Welsh; however Scottish vacillation
and the fiery case made by the Gibraltar representation, together with the
support of the Channel Islands, the Isle of Man, Shetland, Orkney and
the Falklands won the argument for Jebb. At this point England's borders

theoretically triangulated from the far Northern reaches of the North Sea to the distant South Atlantic and encompassed the gateway to Europe's inner sea, the Mediterranean.

Should Europe Dare

At the very end of the opening speech of the English Parliament, Prime Minister Sheagle Wright informed the world that:

> *In the light of the constant build up of Spanish troops near and around the frontier of Gibraltar and the continuing blockade of the Rock, HMS Drake and HMS Warrior are making full steam to reinforce HMS Thunderer in the defence of our territory. We have also placed our troops stationed in Cyprus on red-alert and mobilised twelve regiments of the Army Reserve. This action has been taken in order to leave Spain, Europe and the World in no doubt that we will defend our realm and its dependencies at all costs. We will protect the ties this country has fostered and holds dear.*

The Prime Minister took her seat. The leader of the coalition opposition, Sir Stephen Potts, got to his feet with a degree of foreboding, with the disturbed amazement of the opposition benches for accompaniment. He hesitated, pulled his portly self upright, ironed out his double chins and began his reply:

> *I cannot, the country cannot, the Right Honourable Lady...*

Sheagle was back on her feet to send an authoritative blast against Potts's public school indignation she was so contemptuous of. Legs apart, tugging to its limits the short, tight skirt of her black suit, the garb she habitually donned for Parliament, she twirled to face her own benches:

My loving people!

The Liberal benches roared and whistled; there was a discernable "Go Girl!" From her Education minister, life-long friend and Bethnal Green MP Mithali Raj;

I have been persuaded by some that are careful of my safety, to take heed how I commit ourselves to armed multitudes for fear of treachery!

She turned like a dancer to face Potts, arm outstretched and pointing between his blinking, pale and fearful eyes:

But I tell you that I would not desire to live to distrust my faithful and loving people.

The faces behind Potts were now jeering; some of the coalition was standing, taking swipes at the air in the direction of the Prime Minister. Potts looked aghast at the speaker for help, but no support was forthcoming, the eminent Reg Revins was apparently entranced. Sheagle was in full flow and moved towards the baying crowd opposite:

Let tyrants fear!

She shouted over cheers, cries of "Yea" and general loud approval from her political kith;

I have so behaved myself that under God I have placed my chiefest strength and safeguard in the loyal hearts and goodwill of my subjects. Wherefore I am come amongst you at this time but for my recreation and pleasure...

A dazzling smile flooded over her face as her head bent slightly to one side. Then, extending her small, rounded chin, she turned up the volume…

*...being resolved in the midst and heat of the battle to live or die amongst you all; to lay down for my God, and for my kingdom, and for my people mine honour and my blood even in the **DUST**!*

The English National Party, taking the cue from their leader Roland Edu, stood as one applauding. Potts tried to hold his ground, but was gaping at the raven-haired warrior that stood before him. This Liberal, first amongst equals, was making it clear she was second to none; she paraded, strutting, hands on hips, in front of her foe that were now pulsating like a sea of irate demons:

I know I have the body but of a weak and feeble woman, but I have the heart and stomach of a King...

The E-Co benches began to be vacated as they retreated from the chamber, but some of their number became frozen in fascination as Wright turned back to the Liberals and, spreading her arms out wide, as if to embrace her clan, cried,

AYE! AND A KING OF *ENGLAND* TOO!!

Her loyal troops roared in unison, every one, left and right wingers, all were up glorifying their mistress, the ENP contingent, led by Edu, were united in wild ovation:

AND TAKE FOUL SCORN THAT PARMA, OR SPAIN, OR ANY PRINCE OF EUROPE SHOULD *DARE* TO INVADE THE BORDERS OF *MY* REALM!

She stood breathing hard, her arms now draped at her sides, surveying her jubilant cohorts side on, her black hair had fallen over her face; she looked wild and amazing. She flicked her head to turn, like a matador, at the same time throwing her hair clear of her now fearful countenance. Her teeth were clenched, her azure eyes shot out rays of burning ice, looking at Potts, daring him to reply. The Tory stiffened in her gaze. The entire House was now in uproar; to the extent no one could hear the speaker's appeals for "Order". Raj, a few feet behind her fellow cockney villager, clapped and stamped loudly, she was almost immediately joined by Craven and Jebb;

Tump, Tump, Tump-tum-tump, Tump, Tump, Tump, Tump!

They bellowed -

"ENGLAND!"

The whole front bench was quickly upstanding taking up the mantra:

Tump, Tump, Tump-tum-tump, Tump, Tump, Tump, Tump! -

"*ENGLAND!*"

No one was stopping things now; the entire government side of the House was in full-cry:

Tump, Tump, Tump-tum-tump, Tump, Tump, Tump, Tump! -

"*ENGLAND!*"

At this point Potts knew he was beaten and decided to lead a withdrawal, the only real option open to him. He removed his side of the chamber, some of his now ragged command made token gestures or drowned retorts, but his defeat rang in his ears:

Tump, Tump, Tump-tum-tump, Tump, Tump, Tump, Tump! –

"*ENGLAND!*"

Over the din Wright bellowed;

My Albion will be no piss-corner of Spain...

Our borders will be fouled at the expense of blood and pain!

Tump, Tump, Tump-tum-tump, Tump, Tump, Tump, Tump! –

"*ENGLAND!*"

Tourists outside Westminster stopped to listen and gazed in surprise and delight at the street relay-boards. Londoners on lunch break in the warm, late summer sun joined in, buses in Parliament Square stopped:

Tump, Tump, Tump-tum-tump, Tump, Tump, Tump, Tump! –

"ENGLAND!"

With Glaxco BBC broadcasting proceedings, the chant picked up down Whitehall and onto Westminster Bridge, it seemed that the whole of the City had taken up Sheagle's cause in something of a cross between empathetic hysteria and telepathic euphoria. Kids in playgrounds, chanted at the relay-boards on the sides of buses, trams and trains and students sitting around watching the lazavision at the start of term banged along with the metronomic hymn:

Tump, Tump, Tump-tum-tump, Tump, Tump, Tump, Tump! –

"ENGLAND!"

Sheagle, Mithali Raj, Jebb and Craven waved to their comrades and the lazavision cameras hand in hand. The first battle of the English Parliament had been won.

33

England, & Saint George!

District of Columbia

In Washington DC, Cordy Milne leant on the huge dark desk in the Oval Office and frowned at the lazavision. Laconically he related, "That was Queen Elizabeth's speech to the troops at Tilbury on the approach of the Armada in1588." He shook his head and sighed before adding, "That's one sassy lady". The President, Fay Taylor, sat behind the desk. Her narrowed gaze fixed, seemingly through the figure and into the lazamonitor.

"She's a bastard, Cordy. People who know what they want and mean to get it always are." She watched the tall, thick set, grey haired Kansas Senator hoist himself to his feet. He continued to look at the monitor and as if he was agreeing and disagreeing at the same time stated, "If she's a bastard then she's an English bastard." The redhead leaned back in her huge chair and countered, "Cordy, that's the worst type of bastard." Milne smiled his huge youthful smile.

"Ms President, would you like me to convey your observations to the Prime Minister?"

"Well Milne," she replied, "If you, as my trusted envoy think that would be for the best…" she smiled back at the still good looking if aging politician. She had loved him for so many years and now knew she always would.

Taylor was in the last six months of her first term and understood that any move on foreign issues could end her bid to stay in office, the stay she needed to finish what she and the Democrats had started over a decade before; gun law reform, the final establishment of an all embracing national health service and the concluding strategy that tied America to a long term commitment to harness solar energy, via the moon bases built over the last decade. This would free the United States from its reliance on fossil fuels and break free from the corporations that controlled the extraction and on exploitation of traditional forms of energy, while dictating state policy. Most of all, it would be an end to having to favour Russia and its corrupt business community. In the next four years she and her Party could change the course of world history for centuries to come, but she had to hold off the Republican challenge, who under Senator Raul Juanito, had vowed to take America back to its 'greatest years', which meant allowing capitalism its head, all against all and the devil take the hindmost.

"What is she doing Cordy?" Taylor asked.

"I don't altogether know Fay," replied the Senator, "But it feels…" This mid sentence recess was loud in its silence. He stared at the commercial now being run on the lazavision, a mouse chasing a cat, swiping at the frantic feline with a huge hammer. He knew the word he wanted to use but it seemed inappropriate, although he could not think why. He made eye contact with his President. "Dangerous." The three syllables fluttered, vibrating intimidatingly in the air; like licks of poison fire. Milne and Taylor were one in contemplating the way the conjoined images the word evoked. It gave rise to an indistinct yet disturbing vision, as the sound of the adjective seemed to stay in the atmosphere.

The President broke the spell. "Time for a meet?" She was telling her envoy rather than requesting information.

"Oh goody!" Milne's irony made Fay smile again.

"Well, if anyone can charm the bitch it'll be you Senator". Serious again Milne looked back at the lazavision and said, "I fear even in my best days that wouldn't work with this lady. We're gonna have to work hard on this one Fay. We're gonna have to be *real* clever."

Gay God

The debate about the coming inauguration of the new Archbishop of Canterbury had been going on for some time. Being in his early thirties caused enough controversy but this, together with Lamoreaux Wilbur's sexuality, had thrown the Anglican Church into turmoil. There had of course been many Gay Bishops, but those that had endured had (for the most part) protested and demonstrated their celibacy, at least in the public perception, or been married to long term partners. However, Wilbur was, in his own terms, "a mostly Gay yet bisexual child of the age of gender confusion," who had before and after his enthronement to the Bishopric, openly consorted with several 'partners'. When questioned about this he admitted (or even boasted) to repeated bouts of promiscuity, which although he felt was not presenting a perfect role model, at the same time expressed something God have given him, having caused him to experience, "some of the heights of human ecstasy."

Whilst still an Ordinand at Cambridge, Wilbur, had led Gay protests in the 'Ten percent' campaign that pressurised for the Church of England to legislate that at least ten percent of its bishops be practicing Gays (as Wilbur said, "because practice makes perfect!"). The actions of 'Ten percent' had, at times, involved violent clashes with evangelicals and fundamentalists and made Wilbur a well-known figure in the Press and television. He openly referred to the Arimatheans (a sect many in the Church wanted to believe was more mythical than actual) seeing their leanings toward an understanding of 'pan-genderism' as being both in tune with the nature of the spirit and progressive socially. This led to a wave of speculation about his possible affinity to this cult. Later he became a prime mover in forcing the Synod proposal to oblige the election of a 'proportional number' of Gay bishops. However, when his advancement from Bishop of Worcester was confirmed the news media went into top gear investigating his past. Allegations of group sex and two day homosex-ual orgies with under-aged boys whilst choir director at Cottwest College, were never substantiated.

Many saw Wilbur's shock appointment as a direct result of an e-ser-mon he posted on the 'Gay for God' site. In this he suggested that in Britain politics was the 'new rock and roll' and that the monarchy had become the national religion. However, far from condemning this state of affairs, 'Little Lammy' as he was known to his adherents and opponents alike, approved of the situation, arguing that,

Too long religion has either been so central to the life of people that it has become a massively destructive force, the basis for wars, terrorism and an excuse for crime. It is about time we put religion in its place as a vein running through life instead of life itself. Let the Royal family be the target of crass adulation; let the new 'heavy metal' politicians give cause and purpose to those twisted and limited minds that need to express fundamentalisms. This will free the true spirit of religion for people to live their lives as they want.

There was some truth in the Bishop's words. Over a decade the rise of a younger, more aggressive and attractive group of politicians had led to a kind of popular following that had never been known before. The extension of the franchise to 14-year-olds, following pressure from the influential Youth Parliament, had much to do with this. The YP with its backing from *Solar*, and celebrities from music, net, sport, lazavision and dynoma, had become a force to be reckoned with.

As young teenagers Wilbur and Sheagle had been Youth Parliamentarians. Wright had been spokesperson on Home Affairs, whilst Wilbur took the office of the 'Youth Bishop'. Wright had pioneered the 'Kids for the King' movement, the 'Subjects' festivals and the 'Monarchy OK!' campaign, that had turned the then young King and his then pop-star girl-friend Paramicha into idols, with reality lazaprogrammes, Web-sites and concerts featuring Paramicha.

On his way to becoming Archbishop, Wilbur had become the 'hip vicar' to end all 'hip vicars', leading his own rock band, 'Gay God', that of course appeared at the Subjects festivals. But he had succeeded in hold-ing on to a kind of wholesome image, whilst integrating the Church of England brand of religion into the popular mainstream. Many saw him as the saviour of the established Church, who had brought the youth of Britain into what had been a near dead institution, albeit at the cost of turning churches into venues for, in the main, secular entertainment, with the regular 'God Rave the King' evenings, which had developed the profile of a mass youth cult, with 'Little Lammy', or 'The Bish' as its spokesperson, using the strap-line 'The Kid's Want…' (less school, a bigger government allowance, etc.).

However, a chilly rivalry had grown over time between Wilbur and

Wright. She had gone head-to-head with him on a number of occasions facilitated by the chaotic regimentation of the joint media. For her he had got out of hand, turning seemingly mega-liberal ideals into a sort of power frenzy, bent on controlling minds rather than freeing them. Lamoreaux's response was tell the world that he was praying Sheagle might seek the counsel of the King's Church before critiquing it's servants, suggesting that he attacks were 'surfing on the cusp of treason'. This, of course, made his one time ally Wright an enduring enemy for him and the organisations he was to front.

But Sheagle was not the only one Little Lammy crossed. He predictably created a huge rift in the Church and he had more than his fair share of detractors and down right foes, both inside and outside religion. Perhaps the most vociferous of detracting voices was that of Bishop Tiger Stephenson, the Chair of the Gay and Lesbian faith Alliance. Stephenson continually denounced Wilbur's antics as becoming an over sexualised mockery of faith, a derisible caricature of Gay life-styles that perpetrated every discriminatory stereotype in the book, and of habituating, so at the same time encouraging, shameful moral conduct generally. His position was confirmed when, as the 'Spanish situation' dominated the news-truments, 'The Sky' printed four pages of sordid (although less than pornographic) pictures featuring Wilbur.

Sheagle sat at the kitchen table in Downing Street and over her usual breakfast of fresh fruit, surveyed the coverage with contempt rather than surprise or disgust. She had never liked Little Lammy, or his brand of religion, seeing him as the archetypal product of impoverished middle-class, public school and Oxbridge; the social background that, for her, bred weak hypocrites, stuck in the bourgeois pathology of colonialism. Wright saw the structure of the Church as being hopelessly corrupt in that, as she said privately was, "built on sycophancy and deceit," what she called, "the worse type of lie". For her, the 'lust for status' amongst the clergy led individuals, like those that now surrounded Wilbur, to, "salivate after the adulation of fools".

The front page of 'The Sky' featured the Archbishop naked except for his mitre, but that was the least explicit portrait. The real 'juicy' shots were to be found in the body of the paper. "Bloody fool," she muttered to herself. 'The Sky' claimed the pictures were taken just after Wilbur became Archbishop whilst on tour in Spain. It was unmistakably Little Lammy with a group of very young men. Jebb was leaning on the doorframe that led into the kitchen at number 10.

"What we gonna do?" She asked half smiling. "Apparently there are plenty more where they came from, including a DVD co-staring some furry-friends."

"Too much info at this time of the morning Gwendolyn". Sheagle looked up. "We can't be associated with this nonsense," she said quickly. "We need to wash our hands of the lot of 'em ASAP."

"How we gonna do that?" Jebb frowned slightly as she sipped her coffee.

"We disestablish the contemptuous bastards." Sheagle said without looking up. Jebb spluttered. "What?"

"I want nothing to do with 'em Gwen. The bloody Church has been irrelevant for decades. The truth is, there has been no Church for years now, it's a chain of dodgy community centres, and now this tosser is caught making monk's circles with public schoolboys in his spare time! We need something else. England needs something else."

"You serious?" asked Jebb as she pulled out a handkerchief to wipe the coffee from her chin.

"You bet your tight arse I am," said the Prime Minister. "Serious as cancer. The faith of this country needs to be grounded in the material, not some spooked-up ephemeral entity. It's about time people believed in themselves and not through the redundant, corrupt, middle-class, last vestige of Tory elitism that the Church is. Things were three-quarters of the way there before Bishop Twanky turned up. We're gonna have people believe in us totally, believe in England Gwen and we've got to make this our opportunity. From Cromwell on, the English have despised the Church and all this does is make them right!"

"Okay," said Jebb. Her pale features looking and feeling a bit scared.

"Get the wheels turning Gwen. I want this sorted as soon as you like." Jebb's wide, dark eyes stared at her leader for a moment. She wondered what was behind this. For the first time she felt her trust in Wright waver. That was a bit of a shock in itself. Sheagle had always been the darling of the fight, but now Jebb sensed something she had not detected before in her association with Wright. The former speedway rider didn't like fear. It was a stranger to her. She knew that disestablishment would, by necessity, have huge implications for the way England was governed.

Disestablishment of the Church had long been something desirable to the Liberal mind. Fundamentally it was seen to give the Church independence, to oblige it to make its own way, make its own decisions and this would be an acknowledgement that England was no longer a mainly Christian country. However, the detractors saw the relationship between the Church and the State as at least keeping a moral imperative as part of the Governmental workings, the State at the same time holding the

Church in check, maintaining it in a roughly allied status. Years ago, the monarch had become the 'Protector of faith' rather than the 'Protector of *the* Faith' but the head of the English Church was still the King and as such the disestablishment of the Church would have constitutional repercussions linked to the Monarch also being head of the State; the State and the Church had been made one from Henry VIII onward, disestablishment would change all that, and quite where it left the monarch would be up for interpretation. This in turn would energise ideas about the establishment of an English Republic; State, King and Church becoming separate rather than being the three in one it had been by law, custom and practice.

Jebb was an avowed monarchist. She had been born and brought up in an extended family for whom King was country, and the nation the centre of spiritual reality. This attitude and belief system was embedded in many social movements and popular culture across England and beyond. It was the order of things for millions and the structural means that kept the otherwise multi-diverse entity that England was one body. Jebb had worked all her life to confirm and extend this ethos. The germ of her doubts about Wright had been kindled with the creation of the Kings Council that had paved the way for the swift federalisation of Britain.

"Do it now Gwen!" the Prime Minister ordered, seemingly picking up on the Home Secretary's reservations.

"Yes", Jebb responded a bit too swiftly, "Right away." Sheagle flashed a short-lived smile at her Home Secretary before instructing: "Get on to Tiger. He's a good bloke. Has the measure of Wilbur. He'll help us out with Faith Alliance."

Jebb understood that Wright didn't want any more response from her, but without thinking she provided one, "You know he, Stephenson, has ambitions don't you". Wright turned slightly, clearly giving a moment of thought to her answer.

"Tiger's ok. He's an independent thinker. And we all have ambitions Gwen, including you, yes?" The Prime Minister sucked the air out of any further conversation as she turned and left the room.

The task Gwendolyn Jebb had been given was a job that many governments had toyed with but had somehow never quite got around to doing. When the House of Lords had been abolished many thought the disestablishment of the Church was a logical progression, but the creation of the King's Council seemed to make the task all but unnecessary, the Archbishop of Canterbury being the only 'official' religious representation. But as things stood the Anglican Church still had a place in the England's constitutional framework. While this was maintained Wilbur could hold on to and build on his own influence, authority and power. This said, as Stephenson had remarked on *T4A* a few weeks previously, "Uneasy lies he who wears the crown. Wilbur had done much to effectively make himself a dictator in terms of the governance of the Church. However, all gain has a cost and progress does not occur without a measure of reaction. It might be all well and good to dispense with power hierarchies, but this practice has a tendency to create potentate. The latter provokes the incidence of regicide."

Unthinkable

"She cannot do this! This is unthinkable. Preposterous!" Jose Maria Canizares, Spain's Prime Minister, could not believe his ears nor contain his fury. "What is she doing?" He demanded of Severiano Casillas. The younger man shrugged his shoulders in reply. When it was clear this was not good enough for his Prime Minister he sighed, "The English! When did they not want to rule the world?" Canizares stared at the man who's job it was to 'look after' Gibraltar. He wasn't helping him. "Well, you know them Casillas; your fucking mother is one of them after all!" It was now Casillas who cast a questioning gaze. "I'm sorry Sevey," Canizares was clearly contrite, "But this is all just too much. This hyena is going to war! She thinks she is fucking Drake or 'good queen Bess' or something."

"Look," pleaded Casillas, making settling gestures with his hand, "Nothing has happened yet."

"We can't work on that premise," snapped the Prime Minister.

"Isn't that our usual tactic?" It was now the turn of Casillas to look apologetic. Although amazed at this insolence Canizares decided he needed to make his point. "We have to be seen to be doing something. Remember what happened in the Falklands?"

"This is not the Falklands," Casillas instructed. "We are not Argentina and there is no oil around Gibraltar."

"Then what does the succubus want?" Casillas could see his leader was begging him for a reply, almost any reply.

"She wants the Rock. It was once the key to the Mediterranean, but now it is the wedge that can destroy Europe and bring down an American administration that does not suit Wright." This wasn't enough for the Spanish Prime Minister though. Casillas saw this and so continued. "But the notion of a European state has always disturbed the English; it has historically been portrayed as a threat to England that serves to draw them together as a 'people'. The reality is the English have always been a collection of disparate rather than diverse groups, but have this way of 'coagulating' in the face of menace from 'outside'. At the moment it is Europe, a perennial, but it could be and has been 'the yellow peril', the myth of global warming, or drought." Both men could not help but share the amusement of associating the idea of drought with England. Sensing the mood of doom was lifting Casillas continued. "Wright's position is as old as England. There is nothing new in her stance. But England is more ancient than Europe. We should expect such posturing from them."

"All the more reason to stand up to her then." Canizares felt his states-man instincts kick in. "We must defend European authority." The words spouted from him with all the certitude he could muster.

Casillas shoulders slumped. He looked hard at his leader. He was a distinguished man. His grey hair with its enduring streaks of black and his dark skin situated him in terms of geography, but this was a true European he saw before him; a person committed to the unity of the continent. However, he saw also that his Prime Minister did not understand who he was facing and Casillas, with his English influences, understood that he had no way of telling him. He decided to put it as pragmatically as he could. "For her, she is defending Gibraltar. For her we are laying siege to the Rock. We think she is mad or confused or misunderstanding. She really is not. For her, the position is clear. We think there's a lack of comprehension on her side. This is not the case. It is us who lack clarity and purpose. As long as that continues we are at a disadvantage. Prime Minister, what do you want to do?"

The love that asks no question

He comes to her each night and she longs for the day to end just so she can be with him. He fills her with his spirit, and she is satiated. Their secret is massive, but they love so profoundly it has to be.

Each night she prepares herself for him. She lavishes her body in a bath of oenothera caespitosa scented oils, which echo her Romany spirit. She sponges the warm water over her skin and breathes in the sensual aroma of the candles she has lit for him. Each small ignition, a tint of heat that mimics the small flames of his touch. She lets her hands wander over her body, feeling the satin texture of her skin. She feels she could let slumber take her in this oasis of warmth and aroma.

Wrapping herself in the thickest towel, she pats and hugs herself with the fabric. Small drops of water still drip from her long, dark hair, sourcing tiny rivers down her spine as she moves from the warm lushness of vapour to the edge of the bed they will, almost illicitly, share again.

Wanting to be soft to his touch, she anoints her body with the cream given to her by an Arab Queen. She wants him to be surrounded by the compulsive scent of her fragrance of want; to be caught by her giving physicality. Her fingers massage the intoxicating balm into her calves, her thighs and then up over her stomach. It is all she can do to resist the temptation of her touch, to allow it to slip into the deepest, warmest niches of her physicality; the places where the carnal is transformed into the raw, burning electricity of the spirit. By now thoughts of him occupy every corner of her mind and she can feel the swelling, moist heat that comes from the memories of him.

Carelessly, with a destiny of their own, her hands run down over her stomach and fall between euphoric aching of swollen loins. Ecstasy envelops her and she thinks and feels, letting herself fall backwards onto their bed, surrendering to her blissful yearnings. But she wants to save her passion, her most basic energies for the moments they will be consumed in and by love.

The wind blows the curtains; they are billowing into the room that will soon be full of 'usness', the soft touch of the air breaks her reverie as she moves to the window. She can hear his voice calling her in the night. Her name on his lips! How she loves to kiss that succulent, delectable mouth. She knows that so well and yet it is an 'always new' experience; the delicate flavour punctuates her most lustful moments.

Still naked, she gazes at her body, the body he loves, in the mirror. Tracing a finger down her side and smiling at what she sees. She enjoys how her breasts heave as she takes a deep breath, thinking of him kissing her; the joining that makes them one. With only the gold necklace he gave her for her birthday around her neck, holding the meaningful pentangle, there are no obstacles to the roving of his hands that will want to explore all of her as he makes her his own… again.

The silk wrap on the chair shall be their blanket. The feel of it on her skin makes her shiver. She lies on the bed and waits. Slowly she drags the fabric up over her. The coolness of it makes the small, shallow pinnacles of her carnality taunt in expectant need. She lets it slip between her legs; she feels it pull up against her… it moves slowly on her. She is completely covered. His desire, coated in love will rise when he comes in to see her waiting for him.

Her eyes are closed, but she feels him drawing near. The breeze repeats its wandering through the window, open to the hot, star-studded blackness; the moon is engorged in a delicate scarlet, reflecting their desire. A waft of coolness caresses her skin. She is not sure if it is the breath of the night or his subtle gasp. The silk falls away from her body as she lingers for him with yielding anticipation.

She feels the trace of a finger traversing her cheek, her lips. She wants to take it into her mouth but it quietly draws away. With her eyes closed, she can't see him. She can only feel his presence. The finger continues over her chin and down slowly along her neck. She takes a deep breath as the quiver runs through her. She remembers how his eyes drink in the truth of her. The vibration of his heart, beating quickly, creates ripples in her being; the track of his breath descends in a feathered whisper. He murmurs her name, like it was a being in itself, she is tantalised as the silk moves across her breasts. She arches her back, hurting for his touch. Wanting his hands to cup her, massage her. She longs for him to meet her tenderness with the hot redness. The ephemeral material dropped lower down her body and she is exposed entirely in the pale moonlight.

In this moment she is his, he hers, they belong to each other… alone. Her tactile senses know he draws nearer still. His almost silent voice is in her ear – a husky, beckoning call, filled with an urgency that they are both consumed with. His lips are on the nape of her neck, his hands drift in ductile circles along her horizons. She is paralysed with an eruptive rapture. Her mouth is full of wanting to be filled. As they meet in yearning her body comes alive. She tastes him. She longs to just run her tongue over each hard inch of him, to suck, lick and embrace him totally with her craving vulnerability. His kisses pack her body with waves of delight as his hands touch and lightly squeeze. She must have more of him.

She hungrily bites his chest and runs her tongue along his biceps. Her hands contour the tight muscles of his back, as he so carefully lets his body hover over hers. She is lost in this emotion. She is vanquished in his touch… he slides his hands under her and pulls her to him. There isn't a questioning look. He understands her need… his is a mirror of it… He hungrily feeds on her essence, the soft, caressing, liquid probing, lightly blissful nibbling, as her intense moans grow. Fingers are running down like a rain of elation in the darkness. How she wants to him. Him, just him! They tense, in concentrated, serious play. She pushes her hips into him, urgently longing for the deepness, the insideness, the satisfaction of intense aspiration.

He consumes her like fire, moving down her… she knows his rigidity; extending. She sighs and presses into the bed under her. Enticing him to move lower, screaming in her mind for his heat to reach farther down. She is his goddess, her urgings are his call. He is rewarded with every soft utterance and intake of breath as he lets his passion fall on her. His tongue encompasses her sweetness; tasting the pond of emulsion they have created. Her mind blank, her body moves with a rhythm of its own. Her hands dance in his hair, as the butterfly dances hypnotically on her inner soul. Feeling his breath against her inward, his tongue darting and finding, she drowns in a wave of rapture. A moment is lost; thought or sound is lost in the void of swaying, falling, flying. Only the explosive pleasure exists; he brings himself to her and drinks her, from her.

Her eyes flutter open and she sees him. A glow from the window washes over his body. He gleams. She reaches for him, pulling him to her. He pushes his spirit against hers, his hips between her trembling valleys. He takes her hands and puts them above her head, his fingers wrap around her wrists, holding her there, immobilised by his strength and searing compassion. She slowly incorporates his press into her; they eagerly, but perceptively gently, meld; totally 'coupled'; melted into each other in consummation.

He continues to hold her hands away from his body, so she explores his flavour and smell. She is insane in needing to touch him; compelled to pull him into her, run her hands over him; gently send the tip of her tongue over his lips and then devour them. She seeks out the depths of his mouth, she lightly gnaws her prey as his thrusts inside her quicken. She can't breathe, as her body owns him. The sweat cascading from him drips onto her stomach as he growls a low, dying roar, nuzzling into her. They reel in a spiral of taking and giving. Her hands glide out of his, to contact him. Stroking him, his skin, tugging him into the core of her; she wants to cry out; the desire is like a corporeal resonance in her existence, but she implodes in a shuddering, near silent exultation. She hears herself calling out his name and he responds with the indistinguishable poetry of his overwhelming. She pushes him from her, turning onto her stomach, taking his hands around her until she feels his chest brush her back. She sways and snuggles her buttocks to fit him; taunting him until he takes hold of her outer contours to facilitate their forceful love.

Both moan in the primal desire that overtakes. The urges to just envelop each other grow. His hands reach for delicate pillows now beneath her. She pushes her back into him and turns enough to allow their lips to meet. Ragged panting, strong, longing. Plunging, firm strokes. He clutches her to him and with a final pitch into her innermost depths, he quakes against her. He is hers, she is his. In that suspended moment, what was a 'we', an 'us' becomes one. Phantom lovers that mix together, passion shared, in the darkest still of the night.

Drake

"I know the answer to this but are they still there?" The question came from Captain Eric Chitty, who had just returned to the bridge having taken one of his now famous power-naps (as featured on Glaxco BBC's popular 'Peak Performance' series). *HMS Drake* had been shadowed for the last couple of hours by two submarines.

"Yes sir, still there." Petty Officer Atkinson replied in his jaunty Yorkshire accent. "How far are we from Gib, Arthur?" Chitty was staring out on the dark horizon. "Approximately forty-five minutes sir," Atkinson responded automatically.

"Oh yes, happy Yom Kippur Atkinson," Chitty had just connected the day with the Petty Officer's faith.

"Thank you sir... and the same to you." Chitty looked at Atkinson curiously, "I'm not Jewish Atkinson".

"I guessed you weren't sir, but that doesn't stop me hoping you have a…"

"Yes, yes Atkinson," Chitty was wishing he hadn't opened his mouth. "Thank you."

"All the best from a Tyke Kyke sir," laughed Atkinson.

"That's a tad racist isn't it Arthur?" Chitty was now surveying the sea with binoculars. "Hardly in the best traditions of the service and all that."

"No Captain, I mean yes Captain," Chitty detected the satire but thought his comprehending silence to be the best retort.

Atkinson did say something else, but Chitty was unable to hear what he said above the huge explosion that rocked the entire vessel.

Sheagle Wright was woken from her sleep by her daughter. Robyn was seven now and blessed with both her mother's intelligence and handsome looks. "Mum, I had a dream". The telephone by the Prime Minister's bed rang. Wright looked at Robyn. Robyn looked back at her like a mirror in time. The daughter reached out to the telephone, not breaking eye contact with the mother. The girl put the receiver to her mother's ear? Robyn heard what she had dreamt. "*Drake* has been sunk…"

Within an hour Wright strode purposefully into the Cabinet room to join Craven, Jebb and Rear Admiral Jack Young, Commander-in-Chief of His Majesty's armed forces.

"Good Morning", Wright cracked at the powerful band. "I am not expecting this to be a long meeting."

Craven smiled at the floor, Young stiffened and raised both eyebrows. Gwendolyn Jebb put her hands behind her back and took a deep breath. The Home Secretary steadied herself for what she knew would be a seminal moment.

"Prime Minister" Young began, "My first advice is that perhaps personal feelings…" Sheagle cut him off.

"Personal feelings are not the issue I want to focus on. We have to retaliate swiftly."

"But, Prime Minister" Young interjected, "We have no idea what has happened." Wright leant towards the tall, uniformed, imposing figure of Young.

"What has happened is that *His Majesty's Ship Drake* has been sunk on the high seas. What has happened, Jack, is that we, us, this country, have been attacked and the more we prevaricate the weaker our position becomes. We must hit back now, we must hit back hard!"

"With respect Prime Minister," started Young, doing his best, as a man that had risen though the ranks of the navy, during a life devoted to the service of his nation, it was all he could do to control his temper. Speaking forcefully, but in a controlled fashion, looking directly into Wright's cold and now intimidating eyes, he said, "We have no idea what hit *Drake*. There is little first indication that it was a torpedo. It could have been a missile for instance. The attack did not have to come from a submarine and we do not know who the craft that were tracking *Drake* and *Thunderer* belonged to. So, Prime Minister, who do we retaliate against?"

Craven looked up, "The bloody Spanish of course!" Young turned to the Minister of Defence.

"No one has taken responsibility for the attack on *Drake*. It may have been a terrorist assault, it is Yom Kippur and given our stance on Israel that would not be surprising. We don't know what role the European forces might have played. The Russians have been a lose cannon before."

"Same thing isn't it?" Gwendolyn Jebb said lazily. She raised her head to look up to Young. She was diminutive and lithe, in her early forties, she glowed with the fitness she had always cultivated and maintained. The red in her short, silky blond hair caught the subdued early morning lighting of the Prime Minister's office. "Anyway," she continued, "we've contacted the

Spanish and they haven't even denied they were the perpetrators." Young turned to Jebb, his agitation now obvious

"Sorry?" This was more a statement of incredulity than a question.

Jebb, turning her head slightly offered a fatalistic explanation, "Well, European, Spanish, whoever, they attacked us."

The Rear Admiral shook his head, "I don't really understand that Home Secretary but what about the possibility that it was a terrorist attack, what if there were connections with American activities…?" This last comment brought a moment of tense silence. Everyone exchanged glances.

"We're wasting time," Sheagle said breaking the atmosphere. "I want options now. We can speculate till the cows come home and maybe lose another ship or two in the meantime. We can't let the situation control us; we have to impose ourselves on events. We hit back and we do it now, we hit back with resolve and maximum force!"

Cousins

Since he had become the Prince of Wales, the King had spent a week every year walking the hills of what had been his Principality, accompanied by Freddy Williams. Fred had been assigned to him as his advisor on Wales since the King's childhood, but Williams had also been his teacher, confidant and something of a surrogate father since the death of his own dad. As they sat near the summit of Cader Idris, that – although modest in height compared to its sisters in Snowdonia – had always been the King's favourite hill, Freddy asked, "Do you remember when we camped up here boy? It was a lot of years ago now".

"Yes, I remember," the King said looking out of the familiar prospect. "You told me those who slept the night on her would wake up the next morning either as a poet or mad. I'm never quite sure what the outcome was". They both laughed. They looked silently out over the rolling landscape of mid-Wales but they both knew a question was coming from over the horizon. "What do I do about all this? The younger man seemed to be asking himself as much as his mentor.

"Well boy," the former Wrexham carpenter paused. "The English have a determined lady at the helm. She's not messing about that's for sure. Maybe you might talk to Philip". The King looked at Williams.

His expression betrayed his thoughts "What good will that do?" But he knew the answer he would get to such a question.

"It's what you can do."

*   *   *

"What do you mean he's gone to the Canaries?" The Prime Minister looked hard at Craven.

"That's just it" her Deputy replied. "Him and his old lady apparently."

"Apparently?" Sheagle fired the word back at Craven like a vicious jab. "He's the bloody King Malcolm. We can't have the Monarch just 'apparently' fucking off in the middle of a national emergency. We are fighting Spain and he is effectively in Spain."

"Actually, it is an autonomous region and it's not a national emergency just yet Shelly," Craven felt he had to say something, but immediately wished he hadn't.

"Bollocks!" The Prime Minister was sneering at him with a kind of primal contempt. "The King is the symbolic commander in chief of the armed forces and in time of conflict it's pretty clear his movements and protection are the responsibility of the Minister of Defence. The last time I looked that was you!" The lesson ended with information used, alongside Wright's stabbing finger, "YOU Craven!"

The former soldier looked to defend himself, but he didn't get a chance.

"Don't start splitting hairs with me and acting the prat. This is totally out of order Malcolm. Find the silly bastard and bring him back."

Craven had hardly recovered from being called a prat when he asked, "How do I…?"

"No Malcolm" she interrupted "The 'how' is your pissing job. You lost the little shit now you bring him back!"

*   *   *

The two cousins stood on a balcony overlooking the warm Atlantic that lay between them and Africa.

"Spain is helpless. All the decisions have been taken away. The only one who can do a thing at this moment is Wright." Philip turned to his relative and friend. "Can you talk to her?"

As he spoke Paramicha was bringing them both a beer. "He can talk but Shelly won't listen" her contention was punctuated by a faint ironic laugh.

"How about the Americans?" Philip's query was for both of them. "They hate her". Paramicha asserted. "They know she wants the Republicans to win in the elections. It's all about the oil. England is now oil rich. The lunar energy project threatens all that. If Taylor wins, England loses. It's as easy as that." The men looked at the woman. She shrugged and went on. "And what use is Europe to England now? Wright doesn't want to be part of something, she wants to **be** something. Is it better for England to trade with a strong European State or to dictate trading terms to a gaggle of bickering countries, playing one off against another?"

The Spanish monarch ran his hands through his thick black hair as he replied laconically. "That has always been the English way hasn't it? Why break a habit of history?"

"Yes," the King sighed looking sadly at his cousin. "Fossil fuel forever. The one chance the planet has to clean up its act and the oil companies won't have it."

"But your Eco-Coalition will." As he spoke Philip looked hard at the man who was closer to him than a brother. He knew his feelings about Eva Asquith, the chair of E-Co. Before Paramicha they had grown very close. In fact the relationship was doomed from the start as the King could not be seen to be fraternising with a single political party, particularly to the extent of having a long term romantic relationship with a leading light of the odd coalition between extreme right and left and everything in between that was E-Co. But Philip pursued his idea. "And with some money, and the Democrats have plenty, they could make an impact."

The English King looked back out to sea. His grey eyes fixed on the horizon. "England or the World is it?" The silence that followed allowed the sea a whispering voice.

Paramicha broke the spell. "Roland would be on our side and then there's Lamoreaux as well. With help, E-Co is the one party that could take her on. Just a few words from Asquith and every kid in the country was recycling paper as if by sacred oath. It's an unlikely alliance, but with Roland gaining older voters and E-Col grabbing kids… who knows?"

Elder, the English King's bodyguard appeared. The group looked at the huge but familiar former Coldstream Guardsman. "Craven is on his way from the airport sir," he said. "Seems he's in a bit of a tizzy". His eyes opened wide as his eyebrows raised.

The four relatives laughed. "We'd best not be here," said Philip.

"He knows full well you are here," the King smiled as he shook his head. "I'll see him in the study. It'll be a polite telling off for me before we are whisked back to the centre of Empire."

"Will you be all right?" Phillip looked first at Paramicha and then her husband. His handsome face was intense with concern.

"Oh, of course Phillip. It is you who's in danger. You should go visit Monaco for a month or something."

"No. I will go to Madrid. It is where we should be." They heard the doorbell chime.

"I'll just go and feed the dog," the English King laughed as he turned to face his inquisitor.

Operation Felix

Hitler's Plan for the Invasion of Gibraltar November 1940

Directive

CHEFSACHE
FÜHRER'S HEADQUARTERS – November 12, 1940.

TOP SECRET MILITARY

The Führer and Supreme Commander of the Wehrmacht WFSt/Abt. L(I) No. 33 356/40 g. K. Chefs

By officer only

DIRECTIVE No. 18

The measures of the High Commands, which are being prepared for the conduct of the war in the near future, are to be in accordance with the following guiding principles:

1. Relations with France

The aim of my policy toward France is to
cooperate with this country in the most
effective way for the future prosecution
of the war against England. For the time
being France will have the role of a
'nonbelligerent power', which will have
to tolerate German military measures on
her territory, in the African colonies
especially, and to give support, as far
as possible, even by using her own means
of defence. The most pressing task of the
French is the defensive and offensive
protection of their African possessions
(West and Equatorial Africa) against England
and the de Gaulle movement. From this task
the participation of France in the war
against England can develop in full force.

Except for the current work of the
Armistice Commission, the discussions with
France, which tie in with my meeting with
Marshal Petain, will initially be conducted
exclusively by the Foreign Ministry in
cooperation with the High Command of the
Wehrmacht.

More detailed directives will follow
after the conclusion of these discussions.

2. Spain and Portugal

Political measures to induce the prompt
entry of Spain into the war have been
initiated. The aim of German intervention in
the Iberian Peninsula (code name Felix) will
be to drive the English out of the Western
Mediterranean.

For this purpose:

a) Gibraltar should be taken and the Straits
closed.

b) The English should be prevented from
gaining a foothold at another point of
the Iberian Peninsula or of the Atlantic
islands.

For the preparation and execution of the
undertaking the following is intended:

Section I:

a) Reconnaissance parties (officers in
civilian clothes) will conclude the
requisite preparations for the operation
against Gibraltar and for the taking over
of airfields. As regards camouflage and
cooperation with the Spaniards, they are

bound by the security measures of the Chief
of the Foreign Intelligence Department.

b) Special units of the Foreign Intelligence
Department in disguised cooperation with the
Spaniards are to take over the protection of
the Gibraltar area against English attempts
to extend the outpost area or prematurely to
discover and disturb the preparations.

c) The units designated for the action
will assemble in readiness far back of
the Franco-Spanish border and without
premature explanation being given to the
troops. A preliminary alert for beginning
the operation will be issued three weeks
before the troops cross the Franco-Spanish
border (but only after conclusion of
the preparations regarding the Atlantic
islands).

In view of the limited capacity of
the Spanish railways the Army will mainly
designate motorised units for the operation
so that the railways remain available for
supply.

Section II:

a) Directed by observation near Algeciras, Luftwaffe units at a favourable moment will conduct an aerial attack from French soil against the units of the English fleet lying in the harbour of Gibraltar and after the attack they will land at Spanish airports.

b) Shortly thereafter the units designated for commitment in Spain will cross the Franco-Spanish border by land or by air.

Section III:

a) The attack for the seizure of Gibraltar is to be by German troops.

b) Troops are to be assembled to march into Portugal in case the English should gain a foothold there. The units designated for this will march into Spain immediately after the forces designated for Gibraltar.

Section IV:

Support of the Spaniards in closing the Strait after seizure of the Rock, if necessary, from the Spanish-Moroccan side as well.

The following will apply regarding the
strength of the units to be committed for
Operation Felix:

Army:
The units designated for Gibraltar must
be strong enough to take the Rock even
without Spanish help. Along with this a
smaller group must be available to support
the Spaniards in the unlikely event of an
English attempt at a landing on another part
of the coast.

For the possible march into Portugal
mobile units are mainly to be designated.

Luftwaffe:
For the aerial attack on the harbour of
Gibraltar forces are to be designated which
will guarantee abundant success.

For the subsequent operations against
naval objectives and for support of the
attack on the Rock mainly dive-bomber units
are to be transferred to Spain.

Sufficient anti-aircraft artillery is to
be allocated to the army units including its
use against ground targets.

Navy:

U-boats are to be provided for combating the English Gibraltar squadron, and particularly in its evacuation of the harbour, which is to be expected after the aerial attack.

For support of the Spaniards in closing the Strait the transfer of individual coastal batteries is to be prepared in cooperation with the Army.

Italian participation is not envisaged. The Atlantic islands (particularly the Canaries and the Cape Verde Islands) will, as a result of the Gibraltar operation, gain increased importance for the English conduct of the war at sea as well as for our own naval operations. The Commanders in Chief of the Navy and of the Luftwaffe are to study how the Spanish defence of the Canaries can be supported and how the Cape Verde Islands can be occupied.

I likewise request examination of the question of occupation of Madeira and of the Azores as well as of the question of the advantages and disadvantages, which would ensue for the naval and for the aerial conduct of the war.

The results of this examination are to
be presented to me as soon as possible.

ADOLPH HITLER

*On 19 November 1940, Hitler told Spanish Foreign Minister Serano
Suner to make good on the agreement for Spain to attack Gibraltar,
with the aim of sealing off the Mediterranean and trap British troops
in North Africa.*

Judgement Day – Rota

Operation Judgement – The surprise attack on Taranto – 11 November 1940

The new *HMS Illustrious* joined *HMS Eagle* in Admiral Andrew Cunningham's fleet. They had originally intended to launch the attack on 21 October 1940 (Trafalgar Day), but damage to both carriers prevented this. *Illustrious* took on planes from *Eagle* and launched the attack alone. The task force consisted of *Illustrious*, two heavy cruisers, two light cruisers and four destroyers.

The first wave of 12 Fairey Swordfish torpedo bombers left the *Illustrious* just before 21:00, followed by a second wave of 9 aircraft about an hour later. The first wave, a mixture of bomb and torpedo-equipped planes, approached the harbour at 22:58 and split into two groups, one attacking the ships in the outer harbour (Mar Grande) and a smaller group flying over the town to the inner harbour (Mar Piccolo). The second wave attacked from the north-west over the town about an hour later. During the attacks

the battleship *Littorio* took hits from three
torpedoes, while the battleships *Conte di Cavour*
and *Caio Duilio* each received one, while bombs
damaged a cruiser in the inner harbour. The
Italians shot down only two of the Swordfish.

The Italian fleet suffered a mortal wound, and
the next day transferred its undamaged ships to
naval bases farther north in order to protect
them from similar attacks in the future. The
Italian fleet lost half its strength in one
night, the 'fleet-in-being' diminished in
importance, and the Royal Navy increased its
control of the Mediterranean.

The raid was studied intensively by the Japanese
military and served as an important blueprint
in the planning and execution of the Japanese
attack on Pearl Harbour in 1941.

Naval Station Rota is located in the south-western corner of the Iberian
peninsular, on the Atlantic coast, approximately halfway between Gibraltar
and the Spanish/

Portuguese border. It is situated on the territory of Andalucia, on
the southern tip Cádiz Province, on the western side, between the towns
of Rota and El Puerto de Santa Maria, across the bay from the city of
Cádiz. The installation covers more than 6,000 acres and is commanded
by a Spanish Vice Admiral. Rota is the Headquarters for the Spanish Fleet.

American facilities and services at Naval Station Rota are wide-rang-
ing and diversified. One of the main roles of the base is to support the
U.S. Sixth Fleet in the Mediterranean, supplying fuel, oil, ammunition and

spare parts. The raid on the Rota naval base started just before first light, the dawn of Yom Kippur.

As the early winter sun rose, in three waves a mixture of dozens of Apache and Lynx helicopters fell out of the sky, firing laser guided Longbow, Hellfire missiles, apparently transferring the red fire that seamed the horizon down to earth in a terrible rain of explosive tributaries. It took about twelve minutes to make a huge hole in the Spanish Navy.

The amphibious assault ship *Castilla* was sunk at anchor as were the frigates *Blas de Lezo* and the *Roger de Lauria*. The *Mendez Nunez*, whilst staying afloat, suffered horrific damage. The *Vencedora*, the *Extremadura*, the *Navarra* and the *Canarias* were also badly hit. The fleet oiler *Marques de la Ensenada* was destroyed as were submarines *S84* and *S85*.

However, the biggest casualties, attacked in all three assaults, were the aircraft carriers *Juan Carlos* and *Principe de Asturias*. The latter was left totally disabled, but the pride of the Spanish fleet and the most power-ful ship in the Euro Navy had been completely destroyed. There was also extensive damage to the base, however no American ships were damaged and out of over 500 personnel that were killed or wounded only three United States personnel were injured.

The full light of morning revealed decimation and carnage, but, as the port had no time to respond and could never have expected an attack on the scale of the lightening strike it had suffered, not one helicopter had been taken from the air.

The confusion that ensued at Rota was to be mirrored in the diplo-matic and media activity of the coming day. The first editions in England were full of reports about the *Drake*, most demanding reprisals. The later editions led by '*The Sky*', with the headline 'Crash, Bang, Rota, Wot a picture!' under an image of the smoke shrouded, still smouldering base. This was the scenario that blared the news to the world in a mixture of horror and jingoism, laced with sentences such as 'One back for Tommy' and 'Duffed up Dirty Diegos.'

Milne

Cordy Milne was an Anglophile by nature and heritage. His forebears had come to the United States as farmers at the start of the 19th century and, like his father and grandfather before him, he had been educated at Cambridge. A graduate in history, Milne loved England, its heritage and personality, but he was also aware how both might not be his best allies in the current situation. He met with Wright at Number 10 with the words 'Drake' and 'Rota' filling every segment of conversation and concern around the world. He had sensed a strange euphoria in the air as his car took him from Mayfair to Downing Street. There seemed to be more talking in the streets than he remembered from previous experience and he observed a level of smiling and laughter, the like of which he had not seen before on his many visits to London. People were walking faster, with more… direction.

Milne waited in the lounge for the Prime Minister. He looked down on the front pages of the news-truments flashing on a side table. They were full of jubilation and every hue of chauvinism, from patriotic cliché to several flavours of xenophobia. Only 'The Custodian' seemed to disapprove, calling Wright 'The Goddess of War' and citing the Rota raid as, 'The start of the end of the United States of Europe'. He turned the flicked through the screens, looking for some escape in the sports sections. The coming evening England was to meet France, Italy and Germany in the European

Speedway Cup Final at the Olympic Stadium down in the Docklands. He took in the headline in 'Lions to "Rota Roast" Euros'. He shook his head in resignation.

Canizares

Prime Minister Canizares sat at the head of the huge table in the stately room on the top floor of the Spanish Ministry of Defence in Madrid. Around him were arrayed the Commander's of the Army, Navy and Air Force, the Minister of Defence and Casillas. The group had sat for some time going over the consequences of the attack, the huge losses and the deplorable damage that had been done in Rota.

"How did we not see them coming and why didn't we catch at least some of them?" asked Canizares.

To Casillas, his Prime Minister's hair seemed to have lost some of its black streaks, making him look much older than his 60 summers.

Admiral Conchita Lupue was quick to reply. "There was a general blackout of communications three minutes before the attack. Probably the SAS were responsible, maybe with some 'local' help. Back-up systems were destroyed so Rota was isolated until half-an-hour after the raid."

Canizares lifted his hands from the dark teak table around which the group congregated, shook them slightly and let them drop back to the polished blackness. "But they must have come in from the sea and up from the Rock. What went wrong with coastal reconnaissance?" The Prime Minister was begging as much as asking for an explanation; his dark, watery eyes echoing his pleading.

Lupue shrugged, "We don't know. The strange thing is that the Americans didn't see them either."

Canizares turned to Casillas who had locked into a stare at the reflection of his clasped hands looking back at him from the old polished timber of the table. "Have we spoken to the Americans?" Canizares snapped.

Minister of Defence Santiago Olazabal responded. "Of course Prime Minister, but they claim they were taken as much by surprise as we were. Surely they would have evacuated if…"

Canizares interrupted, "How can so much destruction be done by helicopters?" General Diego Salgado answered, "Well, there were about a hundred of them and the missiles were some kind of enhanced version of the typical Longbow type, but there is evidence that we took some fire from land based ordinance."

"The SAS?" Growled Canizares.

"Probably." Salgado shrugged. "But it was very heavy." There was a pause. Everyone looked expectantly at Salgado. He continued, "It is likely that they've had cells gaining intelligence in the area for some time, again, probably supported by terrorist groups."

The Prime Minister clenched his fists tight. Admiral Lupue added, "It's not unlikely that some, maybe all the ships were subject to SBS sabotage; the whole thing was so precise. Principe de Asturias and Juan Carlos were hit in every wave and in places that ensured maximum damage.

The Prime Minister held his forehead lightly with one hand as he asked, "So how could that be arranged?"

"Some ground level work, inside information perhaps," said Lupue. "But access to satellite surveillance…"

The room fell into an edgy silence. All heads turned to Canizares. He looked at the ornate ceiling and asked the question that most of those in the room were anxious about voicing. "Which could only come from the Americans?"

"Not necessarily." Olazabal corrected his Prime Minister. "The English do have some capability, although information about orbital pathways indicate that they had help from other sources".

"What sources?" demanded Canizares.

The Minister of Defence listed the possible suspects. "The USA has the most extensive network of footprints but the Russians, Hong Kong, Korea and Guangdong also have large surveying capabilities. Of course other nations have more limited means; Iran, New Zealand, Japan, Australia, Canada, India, Pakistan". He shook his head and raised his hands in defeat. "The English could have got information from one or all of them."

"This is all academic really," Canizares remarked with resignation. We have to reply in kind. We tell Wright this will happen. It gives us some honour and it will make no difference. There is only one possible target and they would have already dug in there. We have to ensure we come out on top and show Spain the debt England has incurred has been paid."

Notification

Sheagle received notification from the Spanish government that a counter strike would be made whilst she was still with Milne. This had not been unexpected. Craven entered the room. Cordy did not like this man who had dropped out of Oxford to become one of the best known buccaneering, renegades in the SAS. As he almost half-offered the Kansas man a light hand the American envoy shuddered slightly.

Craven turned to Wright. "Things are hotting up". He had more than a hint of smile as he sad this; jubilation was perhaps the most detectable attitude in his voice. "Jebb will be with us in a moment with something we hadn't envisaged. This is the start of the unpredictable phase. We must concentrate on impressing ourselves on the situation as it develops." Milne leant forward.

With a definite gravity he instructed his hosts, "Listen". It seemed the character of his interjection surprised both Craven and Wright.

Sheagle had thought she might be the first to respond to Craven. "This has gone far enough. You gotta talk to the Spaniards now." This was very unlike Milne. He was the consummate diplomat and well known to English politicians as a smooth talker.

"Is that what you think?" The question came from the doorway that Jebb had just entered. "He's gone redneck on us". Craven was laughing as he made the accusation. Milne was just about the vent his spleen when Jebb continued. "Is that to placate the Hispanic vote in your coming elections Senator Milne?"

"Well," the American replied, feeling totally wrong footed, "If we openly support England the alienation of certain groups might result, yes. You are at least right in that respect Ms Jebb." His gaze was drawn back to Craven. The former soldier locked on to the Senator's eyes. His smile had broadened, almost daring the envoy to go further. Milne had to admit while he despised this man, Craven was as intimidating as a scorpion and he suspected with about the same ethical capacity.

"But the same would be true if you expressed support for the Spanish aggression Cordy", Sheagle folded her arms as she made her point.

"That is also correct Prime Minister." Milne nodded.

"However, there is Senator Juanito to consider." Craven added. "Your wop Republican opponent."

The American took the racist jibe for what it was, another effort to distract him. But his "For sure," didn't hide his clear contempt for what he understood as crass bigotry.

Milne sensed that he had been set up as he found himself making a justification. "The Senator is courting the sympathy of the Hispanic vote, but that means people changing a traditional allegiance to the Democrats." Saying this Milne saw he had been tricked into going on the defensive. Wright broke in.

"We understand your position Cordy. The best thing for the Democratic Party would be if this had never happened. America either intervenes on one side or another; it would be foolish to think that any deployment of US forces could be neutral, or that you might stand idly by. This may win a few voters over, but in effect, as things stand, siding with England or Spain has costs and benefits. It seems the American administration has a decision to make Senator. All I can say is that we are about to defend our territory from foreign aggression. The latter is all we have ever done. If you want to be seen on the side of right then you back us and take a chance with the Hispanic vote. If you stand aside you've probably lost that one anyway and risk being seen as unsupportive of your traditional allies, betraying all our two nations did together to turn the Arab Wars in the favour of the West, keeping Africa isolated and achieving the balkanisation of China… and then there's our joint defence of the oil reserves world wide of course. Where was Spain then Senator?"

Vengeance

The first sortie came in from the sea, from the south. A dozen Eurofighters blazed over the horizon in loose formation, delivering a flock of missiles aimed at anti-aircraft and port facilities. The first thing that was noticeable to the Spanish pilots as they neared the Rock however was the lack of ships and other craft in the harbour. None of the targets they had been briefed to expect were in sight. Nevertheless they unloaded their bombs whilst peppering a range of installations with Mauser cannon fire.

There had been no anti-aircraft response as the Eurofighters flew over Gibraltar, however, a fraction of a second after they cleared the Rock, as if from nowhere, around twenty Super-Harriers smashed into the incoming formation. The Spanish, having unloaded most of their firepower were left with one option and that was to disperse and run, but the manoeuvrability of the Harriers, together with their turn of speed, made the next few minutes into a duck shoot for the English.

As the older Spanish Hornets reached Gibraltar from their northerly mainland flight-path there was not one Eurofighter left in the air. The Hornets had not let off a shot before they were met with a fountain of ground-to-air missiles. The assault was unremitting and deadly accurate. The Rock's ground-to-air defences were much stronger than expected and the aging fighters had little chance of evading or countering the barrage, that included the recent Anglo-American Cromwell 'thinking missile' with its 'Patton' computerised warhead. This was thought by most authorities to be still in its test stage, but their performance was devastating. The Hornets that avoided destruction from the ground were picked off by the remaining ammunition of the Super Harriers.

By now word had got back to Spanish Air Command that things had gone badly wrong. However, twelve Phantoms were already in the sky poised to pickup and escort a twenty strong Mirage attack. The choice was to call them back and come out of the raid total losers or risk continuing the operation in the hope that the English would be beaten by shear weight of numbers.

The final Spanish attack approached Gibraltar from the north-west. This was a last minute change, looking to avoid the kind of anti-aircraft fire that had met the Hornets, although relative to the Hornets the Phantom and Mirages were much better equipped to deal with the English defences. About two minutes from the scheduled strike the attackers received the warning that a swarm of fighters, likely to be Tornadoes, were approaching from the east, across Spanish air space. The Tornadoes weaponry took a toll before the incoming Spanish wing saw them. Five Mirages and two Phantoms were already gone as the English aircraft came into view. They looked like the XL fighters, a heavily armed, long-range aircraft, capable of maritime launch. There were about twenty of them.

It was paramount now that the Mirages, with their bombs, got through to the Rock, so the Phantoms would have to do the bulk of the fighting and draw as much fire as possible. Whilst they were able to account for more than a quarter of the English attack, missiles spent, only three Phantoms were left to make a retreat. Six Mirages reached Gibraltar and did manage to hit several targets, but were wiped out by the combined efforts to the Super Harriers, Cromwell ground-to-air missiles and the Tornadoes.

The cream of the Spanish Air Force, its aircraft and pilots, were destroyed. English losses amounted to eight Tornadoes and three Harriers. The Mirages had managed to sink the Minesweeper *HMS Tiverton*, the coastal patrol vessel *Swanage* and *HMS Oakley*, an aging frigate, had been badly damaged.

There was no hiding the fact that Spain had, in the space of three days, suffered humiliating losses. She had been completely surprised by the scale of England's offensive and defensive capabilities and as such Spain's military intelligence was held up to world ridicule. As a nation, Spain was now severely limited in terms of defending itself. England, having massive naval and air superiority in the western Mediterranean, the troops massed around the border with Gibraltar were in extreme and immediate danger of being systematically picked off. As soon as the level of the Spanish defeat became clear there was a definite expectation of invasion by England.

There'll Always be an England

Fay Taylor hated talking to Sheagle Wright. She much preferred to leave the transatlantic relay in hibernation and instruct Cordy Milne to deal with the woman she had come to see as a hydra. But the situation was such that it had become necessary. Fay looked at the empty study in Downing Street as she opened the lines. This was typical. It would be too much to expect the bitch to be waiting for her even though the conference had been set up hours ago. She thought about the Rock, what this thing, this place meant to Wright. Many years ago, when she had first thought about going into politics, Taylor had read the memoirs of President Eisenhower and had recalled he had used Gibraltar as a command post during the Second World War.

In 1940, surrounded by enemy states, the future looked bleak for Gibraltar. Winston Churchill and the British military leaders believed that an attack on Rock was imminent. The answer was to develop and extend the massive network of tunnels hacked out of the Rock since the British had first occupied Gibraltar. What the wartime Prime Minister envisaged was to build a fortress inside a fortress, a city within a city.

Following the attack on Pearl Harbour, by midsummer 1942 plans for the Allied counter offensive were well under way. Gibraltar was

to play a crucial part in those plans. It had been realised that an inva-
sion of Europe in 1943 would be impracticable, but the allies could, as
Churchill expressed it, attack the 'soft underbelly of Europe' through the
Mediterranean. The plan, code named 'Operation Torch', which was con-
ceived by President Roosevelt and Churchill, was to occupy French North
Africa as a Springboard from which attacks could be launched to drive
Italy out of the war.

In July 1942 Eisenhower was appointed Allied Commander-in-
Chief of Operation Torch and Churchill had placed Gibraltar within
Eisenhower's command as the temporary headquarters for what was, the
first large-scale Anglo American Operation of the War. The American
General arrived in Gibraltar on 5 November 1942 to take over, not just
command of Operation Torch, but also military command of Gibraltar
itself. At his first press conference he had said:

Never in my wildest dreams in West Point days, did I ever think that
someday I, an American General, would command a Force from the
British Fortress of Gibraltar.

```
Operation Torch

One hundred thousand soldiers on the high seas
in a multitude of transports converged on
Gibraltar. Over 400 aircraft of all diverse
kinds were crowded into the dispersal areas
around the Gibraltar runway. Fighters had been
shipped in crates and assembled on the airfield.
Not a cubic foot of storage went unfilled,
being crammed with ammunition, fuel, and other
```

essential supplies. At North Front one hundred
and sixty-eight American pilots were housed in
the RAF messes.

On the 8 November 1942, 466 aircraft flew from
Gibraltar and landed on captured North African
airfields. The 1st Infantry Division, US Army
spearheaded Operation Torch on the American side.

Gibraltar was under constant threat. Hitler
sought to provoke the Spanish Fascist leader
General Franco to invade the Rock and at the
same time had a planned to march through Spain
to take Gibraltar and thus seize control the
entrance to the Mediterranean. Had he carried
out his intentions Malta could not have been
held and Torch would not have been possible.

The British Ambassador in Madrid, Sir Samuel
Hoare, reported to the Foreign Office at that
time:

*The temptation to cut our lines of communication
will be very great. We shall appear to have
put our necks between two Spanish knives [the
Spanish mainland and Spanish Morocco]... The
Germans will be on General Franco's back,
dinning into his ears, "Now is your time. You
can cut the Allied throat, destroying the naval
and air base at Gibraltar and win a dazzling
reward for your country in North Africa". Let
no one under-estimate this temptation, or think
that because nine Spaniards out of ten don't
want war, General Franco might not risk it...*

Many Gibraltarian men served at that time in the
Gibraltar Defence Force, remaining in Gibraltar
to defend it throughout the War (women and
children had been evacuated). They were the
predecessors of the Gibraltar Regiment. Working
alongside the British and American military 24
hours a day to defend Gibraltar from possible
attack, they were also involved in the assembly
of fighter aircraft, provisioning ships, loading
and unloading rations, supplies and ammunition,
in huge quantities in an continual chain to and
from ships and airplanes and in and out of vast
stores protected within the Rock.

From their headquarters in Fortress Gibraltar,
Lieutenant General Dwight David Eisenhower,
United States Army, and Admiral Sir Andrew
Browne Cunningham, Royal Navy, directed
Operation Torch; the first major combined combat
operation during World War II involving American
and British forces.

On 8 November 1942, elements of the Allied
expeditionary force landed simultaneously along
the coastline of Morocco and Algeria.

As such, Gibraltar played a vital part in
Operation Torch and thus a significant part in
the Allies eventual victory.

The evening before her arranged encounter with Wright, Taylor had
reminded herself of what Eisenhower had said about his experience of the
conditions within the Rock. He stayed at the Convent, then as now, the

British Governor's residence, but his operational headquarters were in a small chamber in a Tunnel at the heart of the Rock;

The subterranean passages under the Rock provided the sole available office space, and in them was located the signal equipment by which we expected to keep in touch with the commanders of the three assault forces. The eternal darkness of the tunnels was here and there partially pierced by feeble electric bulbs. Damp, cold air in block-long passages was heavy with stagnation and did not noticeably respond to the clattering efforts of electric fans. Through the arched ceilings came a constant drip, drip, drip of surface water that faithfully but drearily ticked off the seconds of the interminable, almost unendurable, wait which always occurs between completion of a military plan and the moment action begins.

The US President to be had summarised by saying that it was:

...the most dismal setting we occupied during the war.

Yes, Fay knew that it would have not been possible for Eisenhower to tell the whole truth about the Rock; that there might have been good reason at the time he wrote his memoirs to do what he could to understate the potential of possible NATO resources, but his description had meant something. Reading between the lines Fay had taken it that the British had not been totally forthcoming with their foreign commander.

But Gibraltar was vital to the success of Operation Torch. It was the only spot of land in the whole of continental Europe that remained in Allied hands throughout the War. According to Eisenhower:

Gibraltar made possible the invasion of North-West Africa. Without
it the vital air cover would not have been quickly established on the
North African airfields.

Taylor had paused on this sentence and then her eyes flashed back to
Eisenhower's telling summation of the Rock as the *British Fortress of*
Gibraltar. She tapped the expression into the Pentagon search engine and
read what British official naval historian, Captain S W Roskill, had to say
about Operation Torch and Gibraltar:

It is no exaggeration to say that the Rock fortress itself, its airfield, its
dockyard, its storage and communication facilities, and the anchorage
available for the great assembly of ships in the adjacent Bay, formed
the hub around which the wheel of the whole enterprise revolved.

Finally Wright appeared in the frame and, as usual, all in black, sat down
in the ancient leather backed chair that faced the relay. "Hi Shelly," Taylor
started.

"How are you Fay?" Wright smiled back.

"Well, not so good truth to tell." Taylor smiled and frowned at the
same time. "This stuff in Spain is giving me sleepless nights."

"Oh, that won't do at all," Sheagle lent forward with a look of pained
concern, "Have you tried cocoa?? I find a banana before turning in to be
helpful."

Taylor paused and thought 'What the fuck?'

"Ok Prime Minister lets cut the crap. It's about time…"

"Hey!" Sheagle put her right elbow on her right knee.

Taylor stopped dead. No one said "Hey" to her.

"Who the fuck you think you're speaking to?" Fay could hardly believe it was her Wright was talking to. "I…" Taylor wanted words, but no words came.

"This is the Prime Minister of England here Fay, not some towel-headed gangster. You don't tell me to do a thing." Taylor tried again.

"Britain…" once more her thoughts were scrambled by the interjection, "It's England not Britain, and it's Gibraltar not Spain."

"What?" Fay caught the echo of what she had just said, she had said, "What"; for what reason she didn't know, she was still distracted by this as Wright went on.

"Listen, Madam President, England will look after its interests just as the United States will look after its interests. So tell me, are you contacting me to propose military action against England or her territories?"

"Look, Shelly…" The President had lost it; both women knew this now.

"No you look," Wright straightened up in her chair and then nodded her head towards the monitor at Taylor, for the President it was as if Wright was there in the room with her, the 'Supreme Commander' almost felt that the wrinkleless forehead was poking into her face.

"England will not be threatened by Spain, Europe, the United States or any fucker. We are allies Madam President, always have been, we have stood shoulder to shoulder with America through thick and thin. Don't you think we have a right to expect something from your right now, Hispanic vote no Hispanic vote?"

"Yes but…" Fay now hated herself. First "what" and now "yes but"?

"Yes but?" Sheagle threw herself right back into the wings of her great leather chair, "Right! I'm telling you. All the English nuclear subs are at sea, which you of course know and can probably deal with, but also if you move on them it will be at great cost. We have no argument with the United States, but if America commits forces to the cause of the Europeans..."

"This is nuts," Fay had to fight her way out of the corner, "What are you talking about woman?" Sheagle pounced on the question

"What I'm talking about, WOMAN, is the defence of the fucking realm, against ANYONE!"

"Oh bullshit," Taylor hit back, "This is all about oil. I know it. You know it, the world..."

Wright lent forward again. "The world knows shit. Stay out of this Fay. Do yourself, America and history a favour. We have no intentions of letting you lot push us around. You know I'm telling the truth don't you?"

Fay stared at the English Prime Minster. She was ferocious, calculating, tenacious, awful but awesome. Her icy eyes stared straight into her own pale green windows.

"Yes," she found herself saying.

"Good," Wright sat back again. "I think that is an end to our conversation then."

"Yes," Fay felt exhausted.

"Goodnight Fay," Sheagle sat on the edge of the chair. "Try the banana," as the relay terminated the last thing Fay saw was that devastating smile.

Perfidious Albion

Oliver Olson had been European President for just over a year when he met with Sheagle at Chequers. No European leader had been obliged to confront a member with the threat of force before and no matter how well he disguised the purpose of this meeting with the English Prime Minister his task was clear. Europe could not stand by and watch Spain further humiliated by English aggression. The Spanish Government was on the brink of falling and everyone knew that the result would be the rapid break up of the Spanish State, fractured by region and torn between political extremes. This would likely mean the emergence of new and unpredict-able regimes based on ancient schisms, probably producing Catalonian, Basque and Andalusian States, with another possible division producing a Castilian, Argon divide, following a series of very messy conflicts and maybe civil war.

Sheagle strode into the meeting room flanked by Jebb and Craven. "Good evening Olly," she said reaching out her palm in greeting.

"How's Stan," Craven heckled.

Olson hated being called 'Olly', mostly for the because of the image English Deputy Prime Minister and conjured up, it was almost insulting coming from Wright's mouth; it was like being called 'idiot'.

"Prime Minister" Olson clasped both his hands around her fingers. The four stood in a tight circle. Olson was waiting to be asked to sit.

"I will not waste time by asking you what we can do for you Olly." Sheagle smiled as she stifled any trace of small talk. "You have come to tell us the European forces are about to be deployed in Spain".

Olson began to reply but was not given the time.

"You should know that we have no objection to this, given the present instability, but we will insist on a significant exclusion zone around Gibraltar."

"But Prime Minister..." Olson started.

"This is not a negotiation Olly", Sheagle interrupted. "You must understand that any foreign presence within striking distance of the Rock will be taken as a threat to English subjects and our forces there. We cannot allow this. We had considered requiring that the whole of Andalusia be cleared of all but English forces as well as 30 miles of coastal waters, but we'd rather leave such details to European discretion right now."

Olson began to feel angry. "Sheagle..." he tried to offer charm, "You will not put us in the position of having to engage with English forces?"

Wright took half a step towards the tall, blue-eyed Swede. "Oh won't I Mr President?" Her eyes narrowed as she lent into his face, they were about eye to eye. "Let me inform you that this country will do anything, do you hear me... *Olly*? WE WILL DO ANYTHING to protect our subjects and our armed forces, and any threat, Spanish or European, will be met with gravity and resolve. We will enforce a 50-mile exclusion zone around our Rock. You, President Olson, can take that or leave it." She straightened quickly and turned 180 degrees to make her exit in the same footsteps she had arrived in, the regular bumping click of her black high heels 'metronoming' her withdrawal followed by Jebb and Craven.

"But Prime Minister…" Olson raised his voice.

"This meeting is over President Olson," Wright bellowed as Craven and Jebb grabbed one each of the double doors to the room allowing Sheagle to leave like a Caesar Olson was left with the sound of the slam echoing in his ears. He suddenly became aware of having a huge erection.

*   *   *

The next day the European Army began to deploy artillery on Spanish soil. At the same time English soldiers, equipment, aircraft and ships, were withdrawn from the European Army, Navy and Air Force. By 6pm Craven received reports that the European Army were about to deploy its Scottish regiments in southern Andalusia.

*   *   *

Davie Howard met with Malcolm Craven in his offices in the Edinburgh Parliament. He had been surprised that there had been no attempts to summon him to London and that Wright herself was not speaking with him. He was sure he would not do the former but was a little perplexed by and angry about the latter.

"What the bloody hell you doing Davie?" Craven demanded ignoring Howard's outstretched hand.

"What the bloody hell do you think you're doing Craven?" replied the Govern born Prime Minister.

"Look…" Craven started.

"Nah you look here pal!" Howard interrupted. "Ah'll no' hae Madam fuckin' Wright send her Rottweilers up here, tae try and sort me oot!"

" Well, you start sorting yourself out." Craven yelled back.

"Or whit?" asked Howard, "Exactly whit ye gonnae dae tae see tae that?"

Craven calmed himself. "Pull the regiments out of Spain Davie. Do it today."

"Scotland is a free and independent member of the Union and as such its soldiers…"

"Fuck that" Craven snapped.

"Nah! Fuck you Craven and fuck Her Majesty Queen of the Gypsies too. Those troops are part of a European army and are where they are to stop English attrition. And I'll tell ye this, yer bloody subs are fucked too."

"What?" Craven's response was incredulous.

"The subs Craven, at Faslane. The polis have impounded them. The ones that are oot canny get in and the ones refitting and refuelling canny get oot!" Craven studied the grey skinned, bald, fat little former union man smiling in front of him. He smothered an urge to grab him by his flabby throat. Instead, gritting his teeth told the life-long belligerent socialist, "Those are English boats and Faslane was included in the Federal Bill."

"This is a war Craven" Howard explained, his smirk widening, "A war she started. Everything else is bullshit. All bets are off."

"Oh yeah?" Craven asked, suddenly returning the smile. "So, how's young Tony these days?"

Howard hesitated. What had his son to do with all this? Craven opened the brief case he had carried from London, took out the pictures he had obtained from 'The Solar' via M.I.6 and spread them before the unbelieving Prime Minister. There was no doubt that one of the men caught in the frame was the twenty-one-year-old Economics student Tony Howard. The billowing curtains, filled with the breeze of a Madrid afternoon created a theatrical backdrop to his naked son's writhing silhouette. The devout Scottish Catholic swayed, although still glowing from his audience with Pope Adrian VII (the first Scottish pontiff), he was practically overcome with incredulity.

Exclusion

It took 72 hours for the Scots to establish their position in an arc around Gibraltar. 'Scotscure' the infamous private security company that had occupied Belfast in the final uprising of the International IRA, and that has serially crushed resistance in a succession of Syrian and Iranian cities during the Arab wars, took over Algeciras and San Roque. The well-equipped Scottish artillery that dug in just a few miles from the Rock would be a threat to any aggression and be able to initiate and back up a possible invasion. The superbly trained and highly thought of infantry could turn their hand to anything, whilst the Claymore tanks were some of the most advanced on the planet; light and manoeuvrable, but armed with a range of sophisticated and lethal weaponry. The Scottish presence enabled Spanish troops to get out of harms way and allowed the Greek and Belgium forces to be kept in reserve. Things looked even brighter for those who wished to see an early end to the conflict when Craven announced that English forces would not attack the Scottish positions.

However, when Davie Howard gave notice that Scotland's forces in Spain would be directed from Edinburgh and not by Strasburg confusion set in. European commanders wanted to know why such action might be taken. It just complicated matters. The arrival of the *Rhodri Mawr* and the *Gruffudd ap Llywelyn*, two Welsh helicopter ships, in Gibraltar caused even more confusion. However, after a week of bewilderment within the European corridors of power, things became a little clearer. Howard announced that, given the presence of Scottish nationals in the area and the need to show solidarity with Andalucian nationalists, the Scottish forces in Spain would act to protect Gibraltar from military threat, enforcing a 50 mile exclusion zone around the Rock supported by the RAF, the RSAF, the Royal Scottish, Welsh and English Navies. There was, of course, an immediate reaction in the Scottish Parliament. However, the Tory and Liberal parties closed ranks behind Howard, while the potential opposition to this alliance, the Nationalists and Socialists, were divided by the issues of 'Scottish interests' in Gibraltar. There was also the commitment by these same groups to support long-term aims of the Andalucian independence movement that wanted protection for the 'Espano-British' of the region and the removal of Spanish occupation for the furtherance of independence from the Spanish state. As such an untidy compromise to support Howard was eventually reached.

The Welsh Parliament, dominated by Liberals, had with little discord, in fact almost automatically, voted to support the English cause, giving much the same reasoning as the Scotland for its actions.

The news caused the Spanish Government to be thrown into complete disarray. Any European action against the Rock would have resulted in a high loss of life anyway, but with the Scots dug-in on the Spanish mainland any assault would be carnage. There was talk of sanctions being imposed on England and Scotland (the position of Wales was hardly mentioned) but this would seem to play straight into Wright's hands, effectively isolating the island of Britain from Europe. Apart from this a blockade would have taken months to have an effect on the British public, who had thus for done nothing but support the European position.

But the notion was a non-starter. By now everyone understood Wright would not sit back and let England be hemmed in; she would hit out given the slightest reason. Under her leadership the English, Scottish and Welsh navies would not stand back in the face of a threat to effectively starve the British Isles; all concerned took it for granted that Wright wasn't going wait for a siege to take effect before taking action to counter it, which of course would almost certainly be catastrophic, especially as England's nuclear submarine fleet were now either at sea or preparing for action.

The whole tense situation was exacerbated by English demands for an international treaty confirming Gibraltar as English territory in perpetuity. It was made quite clear that there was no other agreement possible as far as England was concerned. The Madrid administration was untenable, being unable to make any kind of move. The European defence system had been shown to be fragile and in no position to fight a costly war with the English ensconced in Gibraltar and the Scots in southern Spain.

The news media in England were in frenzy, not knowing which way to turn first. England and Scotland had effectively pinned down the whole of Europe. A mystery flu-like illness that had laid around a dozen English service people low and claimed the lives of several of Gibraltar's elderly residents was not widely reported.

Hydracraft

Gwendolyn Jebb woke up at 3.13 am at the sound of the rhythmic, mellow, 'Urgent, Urgent' call from her computer. She sat up with a start and looked at the machine wafting its emergency smell of violets and blistering a gaudy rainbow of oily colours around the room. In almost a whisper she ordered "Tell Gladys". The machine instantly checked the sound waves of her voice and smouldered out its secret.

Fay Taylor looked at Cordy Milne, her face like a map of her exasperated anguish, "We got to do something Cordy".

"Chiefs of staff?" Milne looked doubtful at his own suggestion.

"No. We both know what they think. All that 'stand up to the Brits' stuff. Leave it to them and we are landing ten thousand Marines in Cornwall tomorrow morning."

"She'd fight". The Kansas man was thinking out loud rather than pointing something out to his President.

"You bet your ass on that Senator". Taylor said with certainty. "And don't think she might not win."

*   *   *

Admiral Du Casse stood on the bridge of *Le Richelieu*, the flagship of the Euro Navy. She surveyed the horizon. She could see ten of the most modern vessels in Europe dotted around the calm sea. This was just a third of the fleet that had, at the orders of European President, set up a blockade around Gibraltar. Du Casse felt a deep pride at the sight of what was her fleet. "At last," she thought. "Europe had started to assert itself on the English and the 'catin' that leads them."

The thought had no sooner occurred to her when the captain of the Le Rochelieu reported the approach of an unidentified vessel.

*   *   *

Milne looked doubtful, "Maybe we don't know everything there is to know about the Rock"

Taylor nodded. "I suspected as much. The place has been a long time in development if you know what I mean. What might we not know Cordy?" Her voice held a hint of suspicion. Did he know something she didn't? If he did what did that mean?

"We only know for definite what they've told us. The rest is a cross between legend, historical conjecture and the creative application of logic." The Senator said this with some hesitation in his voice.

"Tell me something I don't know Cordy". The President was impatient and her voice betrayed as much.

"You're right about the 'on-going project' nature of the place. Ever since they've been in the place they've been working on it. Christ, it was a hive in Napoleonic times. The Ottomans had plans to blockade it at one point, but ran away, surprised by the response. In 1942 we found out that there was a whole harbour complex inside the Rock, they'd been hitting Axis shipping from there throughout the Second World War; damned fleets of ships turning up seemingly from no-where. The Germans knew something was going on there, even had plans to storm it with Spanish troops, but Franco was scared shitless about that."

"So, you think there's more now?" Taylor was as much intrigued as worried.

"It's almost certain Fay. The place is probably one super huge aircraft carrier, more of a military complex, solidly anchored to and controlling a vantage point that extends over the western half of the Med, most of south Western Europe and a great chunk of North Africa."

*   *   *

"*The Jauréguiberry*? Sunk? Just like that?" Du Casse physically rocked at the signal. "By what?"

"It must be that unidentified craft Admiral," the Captain of the *Le Rochelieu* replied "We have no reports of aircraft or missiles."

"Subs?" Du Casse offered. The captain's reply was swift and certain,

"No trace of subs. Whatever this thing is, it's moving amazingly fast. No ship sailing, of any size can move at the rate it's covering the sea". Du Casse stared out over the water. "The *Drake* could," she uttered.

"But the fusion engines were never fully tested, trials had only made half speed and no-one really thought a ship of that size could stand..." As she listened Du Casse shook her head. The messenger continued; "But anyway, the ship, the *Drake* was destroyed". The Captain was reminding his commander but she had not forgotten.

"The *Drake* was..." she hesitated, "Or is, not a ship. She's a hydracraft".
The Admiral's voice was dead. The captain felt slightly sick as Du Casse
finished her statement. It wasn't the information that brought on this feeling of nausea; it was the lack of a hint of a past tense that scared him.

*   *   *

"Fucking Britannia still ruling the waves eh?" There was bitterness in
Taylor's Irony.

"Worse than that." Milne countered with the resignation of a
scholar of history. "It's Albion's Rock now; England's realm. Britain
was always defensive in character, more about protecting economic
expansion. Historically it was the English who were the Empire build-
ers, using the Scots and the Irish as the front line troops. The character,
the historical culture of Albion, dictates that anything remotely hostile
that comes within punching distance is gonna be splattered that's for
sure. The potential stock-pile of ordinance could outgun all our carriers
combined."

"Well, thanks for the history lesson." The President was trying hard to
resist the tenure of her teacher.

*   *   *

The Portuguese *Sao Rafael*, did not hear of what happened to the
Jauréguiberry, but witnessed the total destruction of the *Jan Breydel* sailing about half a mile to port from her. First mate Paulo Sousa saw a craft
blazing the English ensign, come roaring over the horizon. It travelled at
an unbelievable rate of knots. It looked at first like a ball of fire exploding
out of the sea. Two blinding white flashes flicked from either side of the

vessel and something less than an instant later the *Sao Rael* rocked violently. The bow of the cruiser was covered in a sea of flame.

"Bandits coming in astern". Arthur Atkinson's voice was definite but the volume of the information he was conveying to Captain Eric Chitty did not constitute a shout.

"Right!" Chitty acknowledged. "Turn about. Let's face 'em".

The *Drake* sped round in a tight arc and proceeded to attack the attackers.

"They're Italians" Atkinson confirmed. "Eight Sea-Harriers… in two waves… first wave launched… AMMs away!"

"Yes, from the *Giuseppe Garibaldi*?" Chitty's question was rhetorical. "Best take 'em all at once… we don't want to deal with any more fire than we have to"

"Aye Sir" Atkinson barked

The twenty Blair anti-missile-missiles zipped from the flanks of the *Drake*, destroying the last of the Italian Destructor missiles just 200 yards from her bow. However, prior to this the entire aerial assault force had been destroyed and the *Drake* was bearing down at lightening pace on the *Garibaldi*.

∗   ∗   ∗

"But it was only the *Drake* that did the damage?" The President gazed out of the oval office window.

Milne, standing just behind her, shared the prospect as he replied.

"It seems so. Remarkable isn't it?"

"That's one way of putting it". Taylor gave an effected laugh. "One ship destroys a fleet."

"The *Drake's* not a ship. She's a hydracraft". Milne corrected his President.

She didn't even turn to acknowledge his lesson. "Well, eight vessels sunk, nine more severely damaged, eight aircraft *lost*..." The Senator amazed himself in his efforts to make the best of the situation.

"And the blockade destroyed as the rest of the European fleet hightails it from a single English *vessel* that in effect let them off the hook." Taylor was livid, but at what she would have found difficult to say.

Aftermath

Jose Maria Canizares looked out from the Palacio de la Moncloa.

Santiago Olazabal broke the sick making silence. "We have done all we can do. We are beaten Jose."

The Prime Minister did not turn to face his Minister of Defence. "So we ask the bitch for peace talks and she refuses. She has said all she has to say. She has shown Europe to be empty as a political entity; unable to react to one dissenting party."

Olazabal was looking for some alleviation of his anxiety. His Prime Minister's answer had not done this. "If we give way on the Rock how are we going to stand out against the Basques and then Andalusia?"

Canizares blinked at the twilight bedecked Spanish capital. "We can't. This is an historic moment Santiago; the end of Spain, maybe the end of Europe. We either go along a relatively easy route of balkanization or we fight another civil war. Unfortunately you and I will have little say in what path is followed."

ND - #0222 - 270225 - C0 - 210/148/5 - PB - 9781780914299 - Gloss Lamination